"I never married

Jamie reached up and [...] hand, turning her fac[...] [...]m sorry if I, or my actions, were the cause of your choice."

"Well…" She hesitated, trying to read him. He sounded and looked sincere. Was it the act she'd seen many times before? She really wanted to believe him and make peace with her past.

"I really am sorry if I made you distrust men enough you've remained alone all this time. You deserve a family."

The slight brush against her cotton blouse was a reminder she should have trusted other love interests who came after Jamie. Her hurt had run deep. Now it was too late. She'd be alone forever.

Decades-old anger at Jamie and newly realized anger at herself comingled. "You are the same old arrogant cowboy you were twenty years ago. How dare you think any of your actions affected my entire life?"

Even though it's true.

During the two decades **Rose Ross Zediker** has been writing, her byline's been found on over sixty-six works of fiction, nonfiction and Sunday School curriculum. Rose and her husband live in southeastern South Dakota. In addition to writing, Rose works at the University of South Dakota and enjoys sewing, embroidery, quilting, reading and spoiling her granddaughters. Visit Rose at roserosszediker.blogspot.com.

Books by Rose Ross Zediker

Love Inspired Heartsong Presents

Wedding on the Rocks
The Widow's Suitor
Sweet on the Cowgirl
Reclaiming the Cowboy's Heart

ROSE ROSS ZEDIKER

Reclaiming the Cowboy's Heart

HEARTSONG
PRESENTS

If you purchased this book without a cover you should be aware that this book is stolen property. It was reported as "unsold and destroyed" to the publisher, and neither the author nor the publisher has received any payment for this "stripped book."

Recycling programs
for this product may
not exist in your area.

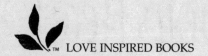 LOVE INSPIRED BOOKS

ISBN-13: 978-0-373-48778-3

Reclaiming the Cowboy's Heart

Copyright © 2015 by Rose Ross Zediker

All rights reserved. Except for use in any review, the reproduction or utilization of this work in whole or in part in any form by any electronic, mechanical or other means, now known or hereinafter invented, including xerography, photocopying and recording, or in any information storage or retrieval system, is forbidden without the written permission of the editorial office, Love Inspired Books, 233 Broadway, New York, NY 10279 U.S.A.

This is a work of fiction. Names, characters, places and incidents are either the product of the author's imagination or are used fictitiously, and any resemblance to actual persons, living or dead, business establishments, events or locales is entirely coincidental.

This edition published by arrangement with Love Inspired Books.

® and TM are trademarks of Love Inspired Books, used under license. Trademarks indicated with ® are registered in the United States Patent and Trademark Office, the Canadian Intellectual Property Office and in other countries.

www.Harlequin.com

Printed in U.S.A.

Therefore, if anyone is in Christ, he is a new creation;
the old has gone, the new has come!
—*2 Corinthians* 5:17

For Jeremiah Zediker, not only because
he has an Aunt Donna, he is one terrific son!

Chapter 1

"Need any help, neighbor?"

A familiar baritone turned Donna Greene's heart into a galloping mustang. A thrill rippled through her, and the hair on the back of her neck stood up like newly set fence posts. She stopped fiddling with the corner leveler on the travel trailer.

Pinching her eyes shut, she used every ounce of her strength to fight the pleasant effects that voice sent coursing through her. Twenty years of hurt and anger should have stymied her feelings. Obviously, they had not.

She called the scene to mind that had haunted her for the last twenty years. The memory kicked up a fury and chased the happiness racing through her until the anger and hurt lassoed her heart and tied down her frenzied emotions. With her foolish heart now in check, she could face him.

A small smile played at her lips. She was pretty sure he did not recognize her from the back. Womanly curves had replaced the willowy shape of her youth. She wore her hair in a trendy bob instead of long and platinum, and time had highlighted the chestnut with strands of silver. It was her turn to take him by surprise, have the upper hand.

Slowly, she rose from her squatting position and turned. She set her jaw and hoped her features expressed anger. "I don't need *your* help, Jamie Martin."

Jamie stopped so fast his athletic shoes skidded on the gravel parking lot. He jerked to a standstill and righted his posture. His eyes widened, and shock etched every line on his handsome face.

In seconds, he recovered. A wide smile deepened the angular creases on his face. A bright sparkle shone in his eyes. Arms outstretched, he took a step forward.

Did he think she'd run into his embrace after all these years? Even if she *wanted* to, and she didn't, she wouldn't. Jamie of all people would notice her surgery had changed the contours of her body. Her fingers found the shirttail hem on her cotton blouse and tugged to ensure it hadn't molded to her chest during the drive.

"Donna."

She stood fixed to the ground like a mannequin prop used by a rodeo clown, hating to admit a large part of her did want to run into his arms. She dropped her gaze in an effort to corral those old emotions. Seconds passed before she lifted her eyes and glowered at Jamie, who now stood with his hands stuck in the front pockets of his denim jeans.

The clearing of his throat broke the silence, but not his intent gaze. "It's nice to see you again."

She arched a brow.

"You two know each other?"

A voice similar to Jamie's, but not as deep, made Donna aware of the young man standing behind him. Had he been there the entire time?

Jamie angled into a half turn. "Yes, this is Donna Greene. You knew her once upon a time, too." He turned back to Donna, his stance stiff, awkward. "This is my nephew…"

"Blake!" Donna clapped a hand to her mouth to cover her surprise and stepped forward. All of her anger vanished. Dropping her hand, she smiled while she drank in the young man towering a foot above her. There was no sign of the chubby little blond boy she remembered. His height exceeded Jamie's six-feet, his frame lean and muscular. "I can't believe it. You were three years old the last time I saw you."

"Ma'am." Blake tipped his hat; blond curls brushed the tips of his ears. He extended his hand. "I'm sorry. I should remember such a beautiful woman."

The right corner of Donna's lip quivered into a half smile. "Ah, you have your uncle's charm." She grasped Blake's hand. Rough calluses greeted her smooth skin. Definitely a working cowboy. "Do you rope or ride?"

He grinned. "Tie-down roper. It's nice to meet you or remeet you."

"Thank you, you too." Donna slipped her hands into the back pockets of her jeans. Blake resembled a young Jamie, except for the blond, almost white hair. His chiseled features and lanky frame no doubt attracted buckle bunnies at every rodeo grounds. If so, it was another trait he'd inherited from his uncle.

Her eyes traveled back to Jamie. The years had blurred the distinctive line of his square jaw and added smile lines around his eyes and mouth even when he was somber. Time hadn't diminished his good looks; it had only accentuated them.

When their eyes met, she realized he'd been drinking in her older image, too. It wasn't a picture-perfect day for her to run into an old flame. She'd pulled on comfortable traveling clothes, an oversized cotton blouse and jeans, run a quick comb through her hair and driven out of the driveway of the family ranch in eastern Nebraska at five o'clock in the morning in order to arrive at the Cheyenne rodeo grounds in time to set up her camper before dark. By now, she must be a disheveled mess.

She lifted a hand to smooth her hair. What was she doing? This was Jamie Martin. Why did she care what he thought of her? Anger at her vain heart flickered through her. She pursed her lips. Jamie should be the one worrying about what *she* thought of *him*. Instead he stood there with a gleam in his hazel eyes.

"Excuse me." Blake cleared his throat. "Could you use some help setting up?"

"Hmm…I think I can manage." Donna turned toward the fifth wheel she'd borrowed from her brother-in-law, then back to Blake and Jamie. "My nephew promised to meet me here and help me get settled. I'm sure he'll be along shortly."

Blake gave her a curt nod and looked at Jamie, whose eyes remained fixed on her. His intent stare made her self-conscious.

She crossed her arms over her chest. The chug of a diesel engine drew her attention to the roadway, and hope sprang to her heart. Could it be Dustin? She squinted against the sun while she looked up and down the campground's road hoping to spy Dustin's white pickup.

A black pickup turned the corner, and Donna held in her disappointed sigh. She'd stayed away from rodeo arenas for twenty years all because she didn't want to run into Jamie. But Dustin was on a winning streak, so she'd put aside her fear to cheer him on. This might be his year to make it all the way to the National Finals.

Then something clicked in her brain. "Did you say you were a tie-down roper?"

"Yes, ma'am."

"He's third in points standing. If he does well here at the Daddy of 'em All, he'll take the lead over Dustin Bliss. This is his year. He's building steam to go the National Finals in December."

Jamie slipped easily into his announcer voice. Rattling off information on his nephew's career the way he would if he were behind a microphone talking to a roaring crowd. He patted Blake's back, pride shining from his face.

"I don't know." Donna lifted her brows. "Dustin Bliss is a very good roper."

"Yes he is, but I really think I might be able to beat him." Hope filled Blake's voice.

"I told you." Jamie wagged his index finger at Blake. "There's no might about it. You will beat him."

Donna shook her head and smiled at the men. "Well, best of luck to you." The sport of rodeo was a fierce competition that took talent, ability and luck. And for tie-down ropers and steer wrestlers, a well-trained horse. She'd root for her nephew, but she didn't wish harm or loss to any cowboy. Plus she'd been around cowboys all of her life and the top athletics all had one thing in common: self-confidence.

"Let us help you. Your nephew might be tied up unloading the…" Jamie lowered his head. In a voice barely audible he finished his sentence. "Stock."

His whispered word roiled her age-old anger. Jamie's attempt at remorse didn't fool her. She'd witnessed his please-forgive-me act more than one time in her life.

"I doubt it." She spat out the words.

Blake took a step back.

Jamie's signature brown Stetson brim slowly rose. His regret-filled eyes beseeched hers. Sadness etched the plains of his face.

She almost snorted like a cinched bull. He'd honed his skills over the years—body language, facial expression. Next would come the pleading voice. She crossed her arms over her chest, narrowed her eyes and waited.

The silent air between them filled with tension heavier than the July humidity she'd left behind in Nebraska.

"Oh!"

She transferred her gaze from Jamie to Blake's wide eyes and stunned expression. He'd figured out who she was and how she and Jamie knew each other.

Her heart softened. For three years she'd loved the little boy inside the young man standing before her. At one time she'd considered him her family, called him her nephew. After she and Jamie broke up, she'd missed the little towhead until her sister delivered Dustin. Then she poured out all of her love on her godson.

"Thank you for your offer, but…"

"We're not taking no for an answer." Jamie's firm voice sliced through the tension. He nodded toward Blake. "You start in back and I'll do the front."

Jamie pushed past Donna.

"I said no." Her body tensed. She fisted her hands by her sides.

Blake hesitated until Jamie turned around. "It's the cowboy thing to do. If your nephew gets here, we'll stop and let him finish up. Right now, neither of us is going to let a lady set up camp by herself."

She opened her mouth to protest, then reconsidered. Jamie owed her and her family. Securing her travel trailer and cranking out her sliders was a measly down payment for everything her family had lost.

Standing back, she watched the two men efficiently working together. Donna seized the opportunity to really look at Jamie. Twenty years ago, Jamie's build resembled Blake's, lean and lanky. Time had thickened his core and rounded the edge off his shoulders and chin, but for a man in his midforties, he was fit. His physique would still turn heads. Unlike in their youth, he wore a blue pocket-front T-shirt tucked into carpenter-style jeans instead of a plaid Western shirt and deeply creased Wrangler jeans. Athletic shoes replaced the pointed-toe cowboy boots. The only remnant of his past attire was his felt Stetson.

"That should do it." Jamie lifted his hat and wiped his forearm across his brow. His short brown hair was flat and matted from the warmth of the felt hat. A straw cowboy hat would be so much cooler in the July sun, but Jamie had always preferred the look of felt.

"Thank you. I have soda in a cooler in the back of the pickup box. Help yourself." She didn't really want to socialize with Jamie. Offering them a beverage was the polite and Christian thing to do after he and Blake had exerted themselves in the warm sun. Besides, there was a fifty-fifty chance they'd turn her down.

"Sounds good." Blake reached over the end gate and lifted the cooler's lid.

So much for her chances.

"Anyone else?"

"Sure, any flavor is fine." Jamie sat his hat on his head then slid it back exposing his forehead.

"I'm glad because there is only one kind in there." Donna shrugged.

"Let me guess." Jamie lifted a finger to his temple and tapped it as if he were pondering a guess. "Root beer?"

"Old habits die hard." Donna smiled and shrugged again.

"I've heard cowboys talk about your bull." Blake handed Donna, then Jamie, a can of soda. "They say he's one fierce hombre. The Brahma must be giving your nephew quite a time unloading or he'd be here by now." Blake pulled the tab on the aluminum can. A shush of air punctuated his statement. A small spray of sticky liquid scented the air with vanilla.

"Antagonist is a mean one. His twists, turns and spins come natural. He was sired from one of the best. We have high hopes for him making it to the National Finals, just like we did…"

Donna's voice trailed off at the sag of Jamie's shoulders.

She cleared her throat and gave him a pointed look. "But that isn't what's keeping this nephew. My brother, Cameron, runs the rodeo stock contracting company. The nephew I'm waiting for is my sister Deanne's, son."

"I remember her being sweet on one of your hired hands." Jamie chuckled. "Did he finally return her affections?"

"No." Donna shook her head. "Twenty years ago, she met a cowboy during the summer rodeo season. They were married by Christmas."

"Good for her. Who was the lucky cowboy?"

"Harrison Bliss."

The look on Jamie's face when he filled in the gap was priceless. Donna didn't try to hide her sly smile.

"Dustin Bliss is your nephew?"

"Dustin Bliss is your nephew!" Blake removed his straw cowboy hat and swatted it against his thigh. "What a small world. Don't you think so, Uncle Jamie?"

Jamie took a long swig of root beer. Anything to keep his reaction in check to the little bombshell Donna had dropped. All this time they'd stood here visiting, Donna had known her nephew was Blake's main competition.

Although he told Blake to be positive, Jamie knew Blake's biggest hurdle to overcome for the championship title was Dustin. No wonder Dustin was a force to be reckoned with; his dad, the son of a Texas oilman, had been a champion tie-down roper in his prime, and his mom was a prestigious equestrian trainer. Dustin, a pilot, flew to rodeos, which saved time and increased the number of rodeos he competed in. Dustin wore shirts with his sponsor's logo, but he certainly didn't need a sponsor to help him work the circuit. Even without a sponsorship, Dustin would have had enough family money on the Bliss side to make it to all the big and small rodeos whether he won or not.

On the other hand, Blake needed a sponsorship, and with his surge in winnings, Jamie had prayed nightly for it to happen. His winnings had to support his travel to the next rodeo. Blake had skill, although when the stakes were high, his confidence waivered.

Jamie had been wearing out his knees praying for his nephew's success. Now he guessed more prayer time was in his future. But who was he kidding? His aggravation at Donna and need for extra prayer time had nothing to do with their nephews. Of all the RV parking spots in Cheyenne, theirs had to be next to each other. He thought time had dimmed his attraction to her. Seeing her again made it burn brighter than ever.

She'd always been attractive. But the way her womanly curves filled out her jeans and her hair framed her lovely face with its natural color made her irresistible. Divine intervention would be the only thing to keep him from acting on his feelings, something he couldn't do. He needed to seek out forgiveness from Donna and her family. It was a step in his recovery he'd never been man enough to complete.

"Uncle Jamie? What do you think?"

Blake's question popped him back to the present conversation. "I'm sorry, what?"

"I invited Donna and Dustin to supper. She thinks you might not go for the idea. It is all right, isn't it?"

Donna's wide-eyed expression and slight shake of her head pleaded with Jamie to make an excuse, say no. He completely understood. Sharing a meal with him would be uncomfortable for her at best.

He cleared his throat while looking from Donna to Blake. "I don't see why not, it's nothing fancy, grilled hamburgers and potato chips." When he looked back at Donna he received the reaction he expected, pinked cheeks and a narrow-eyed stare. Some things about her had changed. Not everything. She always did look pretty when riled up.

"So what do you say?" He felt a cocky smile play at his lips. He fought it. He didn't want to goad her since he'd cornered her like a calf backed in the chute before the roper gives a nod. In order to make amends Jamie needed to break the barrier, and the only way to do it was to spend time with Donna and her family.

"I can't really speak for Dustin…"

"About what?" A deep Southern drawl came from behind them.

"Dustin!" Donna opened her arms to the thin young man.

A pang of jealousy twisted through Jamie. She'd ignored his outstretched arms. But why wouldn't she? He'd instinctively reached out, hoping time had dulled her pain and anger. He should have known better.

"This is Jamie and Blake Martin. They have invited us to dinner."

Dustin clasped Blake's outstretched hand. "I don't know. He's the competition." A broad smile accompanied his teasing words. "It's nice to see you again."

The smile faded when Dustin turned to Jamie. "Mr. Martin."

His greeting and overly strong handshake were brief. Dustin's message came through loud and clear. Amends with any branch of the Greene family wasn't going to be easy.

"We'd love to have you join us." Jamie sincerely wanted them to be his dinner guests, no matter the meager offerings. He wanted to make amends, needed to make amends. Besides, he was curious to find out what Donna had been doing all these years. Would she be surprised to find out how his life had turned out?

"What do you say, Aunt Donna?" Dustin stepped to her side and wrapped a protective arm around her shoulders.

"It'd sure be an honor if you'd join us." Blake smiled, hope evident in his expression.

Donna drew a deep breath. Her features softened with her audible exhale. "Okay, it would be nice after a long day on the road."

"Great, I'll go get the grill started." Blake turned to go. Jamie knew he should join him, but his heart was reluctant to leave Donna, even for a few minutes.

"Just a second," Donna said.

Blake stopped and turned back to her.

"I have items to contribute to dinner. I have some fresh veggies, would you mind grilling those?"

"Not at all, ma'am."

"Please call me Donna."

Jamie envied the soft look she gave Blake.

Dustin looked around. "Since your camper's set up, guess I'm not needed here. I'll grab the veggies and help cook." Lips locked in a grim line, he shot Jamie a hard look. "You don't mind do you, Aunt Donna?"

Glancing at Jamie, she gave Dustin a weak smile. "I don't mind."

Several minutes later, he and Donna stood two feet apart watching their nephews round the end of Jamie's camper.

Tension-filled silence surrounded them. Finally, Donna cleared her throat. "I suppose there's no chance you can get another camping spot?"

Her raised brows widened her caramel-colored eyes. Her eyes used to shine with love for him, now they expressed her smoldering anger and hurt. Along with a flicker of something else. Fear?

He shrugged. "I'm sure they're all filled up."

"Surely you know someone to trade spots with." Donna crossed her arms over her chest.

Jamie shook his head. "It's only for a short time."

"Almost two weeks. Unless you're leaving before the rodeo is over?"

Disappointment cut through him at Donna's hope-filled question. Seeking the Greenes' forgiveness, especially Donna's, was going to be more difficult than he'd imagined. And over the years, he'd imagined the worst.

Shifting his weight from one foot to the other, he watched the hope creep from her face with a small shake of his head. "Nope, we're here for the duration."

Chapter 2

"I think they might become friends more than competitors." Jamie lifted his hand giving the drivers in the departing pickups a small wave.

"Hmm…" Donna stared into the dusky void left by Blake's vehicle.

She'd engaged in conversation with Blake and Dustin during their picnic dinner, however when Jamie addressed her, she'd given one- or two-word answers. Now that they were alone, sitting side by side in the lawn chairs, her answers were reduced to a hummed response.

Maybe it was the July heat. Maybe it was his emotional state at being near Donna again. Maybe it was because he was weak. His body yearned for the one thing he couldn't have: an icy cold beer. It'd give him the courage he needed to iron out their past.

He hung his head the instant the thought popped into his mind. It'd give him bravado all right, false bravado.

Rolling his wrist, he checked his watch. Over twelve hours until Grant, his sponsor, arrived. Could he make it that long? He put the plastic bottle he held to his lips and took a long drink. The water hydrated his body, but didn't quench his thirst. If Donna would only talk to him, it might get his mind off alcohol.

Jamie drew a deep breath, the ragged intake the only noise between them. It was a risk to lead with the apology. Small talk wasn't working and purging his guilt might ease his yearning for a drink.

"Thank you for dinner."

Donna's words rushed out. Her instincts must have told her he wanted to talk. What they didn't tell her was he *needed* to talk. Now wasn't the time for him to be alone.

She placed her hands on the armrests of her chair, pushed up and took a step.

"Don't go." Jamie grabbed her hand, hating the desperation in his voice, loving the silkiness of her skin. Unable to help himself, he caressed her hand with the pad of his thumb.

She wrinkled her brow and frowned. "I don't really think we have anything to say to each other." She tried to tug her hand free.

"That's not true." He tightened his grip. "We have a lot that needs to be said. Please sit down. I want to apologize."

"I've heard it all before." Her loud, dramatic sigh echoed through the night. After a short pause, she sat back down and stared vacantly at the neighboring RV.

"Yes, you did, when it wasn't sincere. I was arrogant…"

"You can say that again." Donna turned to him, her face defiant.

Emotion shook his insides. Man, one drink would take the edge off, help him get through this conversation. He licked his dry lips. He needed to keep her with him until this urge passed.

"I know what I did to you and your family is hard to forgive. I'm so sorry it happened. If I could turn back time, make everything right, I would. Please believe me. I live with the regret every day of my life. Can you ever forgive me?"

Her eyelids fluttered before she puckered her brows. She looked off into the distance, sighed and turned back to him. The curtain of defiance covering her pretty brown eyes had left yet her stare remained hard. "Against my better judgment I do believe you're truly sorry this time. But I don't know if I can ever forgive you."

His shoulders sagged. He slid down a few inches in his chair and gulped more water. With a swallow harder than necessary for the lukewarm liquid, he seized what might be his only opportunity.

"Donna, please forgive me. I've changed. I'm trying to make amends. Is there anything—" He leaned forward, placing his hand on her arm. When she didn't pull away, reassurance washed through him, helped him to continue. "—I can do to get you to forgive me?"

The warmth of the soft skin beneath his rough palm steadied his shaking insides. His touch on Donna's skin fortified him, gave him strength.

"I don't know." She placed her hand on top of his, moving it from her arm to the armrest of his lawn chair.

Although the comfort of her touch was gone, the strength remained. Jamie sat straighter. Her voice and body language weren't encouraging, but they weren't hostile either. Her face registered a faraway look. Was she remembering the good times they'd had in the past? Or the bad?

"Give me until the end of Frontier Days to prove it to you." He held out his hand.

She sighed. "All right."

Donna ran her fingers through her hair, sticking a clump behind her right ear before she slipped her hand into his, clamping down tight. "It's time for both of us." She released his hand and stood. "Good night."

Jamie stood. "I'll walk you to your trailer."

"There's really no need." Donna rubbed her hands up and down her bare arms. The white sleeveless blouse she wore provided little protection in the cool night air.

"Yes, there is." Jamie held up his hands at the sharp look Donna shot him. "I'll stop at the end of my trailer and watch until you are safely in yours." He took a step and held his hand out for Donna to walk in front of him.

Faint laughter danced through the evening air filling the silence between them while they walked the length of his camper, their moonlit shadows leading the way. Staying true to his word, Jamie stopped when they rounded the end of his trailer. "Good night."

Donna gave him a small smile. "Good night."

Jamie watched her stride to her RV door, then disappear inside. Absently he played with his water bottle. By giving him the benefit of the doubt, she'd temporarily quenched his thirst for other beverages.

Closing her book of devotions, Donna lifted her coffee cup, then lowered it again. What did the last passage say? She'd absently read her Bible today. Her mind was on other things, other people. Opening it to her book mark, she reread the verse in 2 Corinthians 5:17, "Therefore if anyone is in Christ, he is a new creation; the old has gone, the new has come!"

She wrinkled her brows, absorbing the message of the text. She put her mug to her lips and took a sip. She cringed, swallowing the room-temperature java. Frowning, she stood and walked the two steps from her love seat to the kitchen sink.

Emptying the cold coffee down the drain, Donna peeked out the small window at Jamie's trailer. To her surprise, it'd been a quiet night at her neighbor's campsite. The Jamie she used to know would be calling it a night right about now. Had he changed? He did seem different.

Pushing her fingers through the space between the buttons of the red bandanna-print blouse she'd paired with rhinestone-studded jeans, Donna rubbed the skin two inches below the right side of her collar bone where the scar started.

A year ago she planned to come to terms with her regrets, which included Jamie and her decision to play it safe and live the only kind of life she knew instead of pursuing the exciting life she'd dreamed of in her youth. She'd managed to put all of her emotional business in order except Jamie. At the time, she considered trying to find him. But in the rush of presurgery, surgery, and postsurgery, the notion was forgotten.

After a few months, relieved when the doctor had given her a clean bill of health, it no longer seemed important. She settled back into her comfortable life. Of all the things she'd vowed to do, going to church and forming a closer relationship with God was the only promise she kept. Now a tickle of regret niggled within her at settling for a safe life.

Jamie had been so earnest in his request for forgiveness last night, she wondered if he was having health issues of his own.

Lifting her cell phone, she checked the hour. There were many ways to spend your time at the Daddy of 'em All besides watching the rodeo competition and she planned to take in the other activities: shopping, parades and the midway. Right now, though, she needed to start walking to the campground's entrance where Dustin would pick her up. He would drop her off at Frontier Park since her brother needed to use her pickup today. She didn't want to be late for her volunteer training session with the Fellowship of Christian Cowboys.

She slipped her phone in her purse, grabbed a small pad of paper in case she needed to take notes during training and headed out of her door. She walked to the end of her camper. Looking down the street to her left, she turned to the right—and bumped into Jamie.

"Whoa, pony. I mean filly." Jamie caught her shoulders to help her keep her balance.

The merriment dancing in his hazel eyes at his lame joke tugged a smile to her lips.

"Sorry. I'm trying to figure out the quickest route to the entrance." Donna glanced around the RV park.

"It's this way. I'll walk with you. I could use the exercise."

Spending more time with Jamie wasn't a part of her plan today, but since she was running late, she'd accept his help. "Okay." She shrugged her shoulders and realized Jamie's hands still rested there.

"Hmm…" Donna raised her brows and jerked her head toward his hands. "I don't think there is a risk of my falling over anymore."

Jamie pulled his hands back. His cheeks pinked. Donna's heart picked up pace. She leafed the pages of the paper pad to give her hand something to do other than reach up and caress his freshly shaven face, one of her favorite things to do once upon a time.

That kind of thinking had to stop. She waved a hand through the air. "Lead the way." Perhaps physical movement would stop her nostalgic feelings.

"It's this way and good morning." Jamie's voice cracked a little. He cleared his throat. "Guess I haven't had enough coffee yet."

"Good morning." Donna smiled. Jamie was fully decked out in cowboy clothes, from the crown of his black felt cowboy hat to the silver toe tips on his boots. Black embroidered Celtic crosses adorned the front and back yokes of his white Western-cut shirt. The crease in his dark jeans, a shade or two lighter than the rest of the pants, drew a neat line to the pointed toe of his black cowboy boots.

Her cantering heart pounded in her ears. She drew a steadying breath and forced her gaze forward.

A few inches separated them as they walked side by side, the scuff of Jamie's boot heels on the blacktop surface the only conversation.

To fight the urge to steal sideways glances in order to memorize his older, handsomer image, Donna focused her attention on the rows of campers, all shapes and sizes, lining the asphalt road of the campground. A few spots remained open. Donna was certain they'd be occupied by nightfall. A faint breeze wafted smoky bacon, strong coffee and warm cinnamon aromas from the open windows of the trailers they passed.

Jamie broke the silence. "A penny for your thoughts."

* * *

"I'm thinking." Donna tilted her head sideways. "I should have eaten breakfast with these people instead of having my usual instant oatmeal."

"It does smell good." Jamie lifted his brows. "I have oatmeal every day. Cholesterol problems."

"My numbers are good." Donna kicked a rock with the square toe of her red leather boots. "I just love oatmeal's creamy texture."

"My cholesterol problem goes hand-in-hand with my high blood pressure, or so the doctor tells me." Jamie rubbed his chin with his thumb and index finger as if he was contemplating the truth of his diagnosis.

"I don't suffer from either of those ailments." Donna stuck some strands of hair behind her ear. Her giggle cut through the quiet morning.

"What's so funny?"

"Discussing our health issues. We're not *that* old."

A hearty laugh bounced out of Jamie. "Let's change the subject. Tell me what you've been doing the past twenty years."

She wasn't certain she should let her guard down around Jamie. Besides, he knew the big plans of her youth—an exciting life which included travel to exotic locales. It was hard to admit that after she broke up with him, she stayed on the ranch, found a safe career in a familiar place and visited exotic lands from the comfort of a classroom with her travel club. "Not much. Just living life I guess."

She stopped at an intersection.

"Your answer's pretty ambiguous." Jamie motioned the direction with his index finger.

Turning to her right, Donna could see the entrance gate about three blocks away.

"Do you work for your brother, running the lives to…" Jamie stopped, and cleared his throat. "Family business?"

"No." She had wanted to. Her dad and Cameron wouldn't allow it. "I'm the director of the marketing department at the University of Nebraska. I still live on the family ranch. Although I built my own house, closer to the highway."

Heat burned her cheeks at the monotone way she delivered the details of her life. Why did she suddenly feel ashamed of her life? Her job was fulfilling and respectable. However, it wasn't the plan she'd mapped out for her future. "Is that the information you wanted to know?"

"Not really."

She caught the small shake of his head in her peripheral vision and frowned at his response. "Your turn."

"I'm still a PRCA announcer. I work with a couple of small outfits. I travel on the summer circuit with one company. I do a few winter rodeos with the other. I own a small spread in northern California, and…"

The dip of her heart forced out her astonishment, interrupting Jamie. Coughing, she stopped walking and lifted her fingers to her lips. Twenty years ago, she'd thought her plan to see her dreams come true was concrete—unlike Jamie's pipe dreams. Yet he'd made his come true. And she had not.

"Are you okay?" In an instant, Jamie clasped her free hand. Concern clouded his eyes.

"Yes, I must have swallowed wrong or something. I'm really glad you made it to California." She thought those words would be harder to say. Turned out they weren't. She was okay with the fact Jamie had pursued his life's goal.

Jamie rewarded her with a weak smile. He pulled his long fingers down the length of her hand before letting go. Warm ripples tingled up her arm.

"I'm judging by the bare ring finger on your left hand, you aren't married."

She found a focal point and kept her eyes directed on it. She wasn't sure where he was going with that question, and even though she should, she couldn't look at him. Either way it didn't make answering him any easier. She cleared her throat. "No, I'm not."

"Were you ever?"

Why was he doing this? But she knew why. She'd contemplated doing it herself a year ago. Donna stole a sideways look. Jamie stared straight ahead, also focusing on the far-off horizon.

Was he fighting emotions too? Somehow thinking he was, made it easier for her to answer. "No, I never married."

Jamie reached up and cupped her cheek with his hand, turning her face to him. "I'm sorry if I, or my actions, were the cause of your choice."

"Well." She hesitated trying to read his body language. He sounded and looked sincere. Was it the act she'd seen many times before? She really wanted to believe him and make peace with her past.

"I really am sorry if I made you distrust all men enough you've remained alone all this time. You deserved a family."

Donna secured her purse on her shoulder and crossed her arms over her chest. The slight brush against her cotton blouse was a reminder she should have trusted other love interests who came after Jamie. Her hurt had run deep. She'd kept them all at arm's length until they grew disinterested and moved on. Now, it was too late. She wouldn't even try a serious relationship. She'd be alone forever.

Decades-old anger at Jamie, and newly realized anger at herself, comingled creating a force fiercer than Antagonist. "You are the same old arrogant cowboy you were twenty years ago. How dare you think any of your actions affected my entire life?"

Even though it's true.

The truth clogged her throat, stopping her tirade. She paused, angrier at herself than she was at Jamie. Yet after the stunt he'd pulled twenty years ago, didn't he deserve the treatment he was receiving?

Hurt settled in the crevices of Jamie's face. He jutted his chin out, lifted a hand and ran his fingers up and down the skin of his cheek. Her words had delivered the figurative punch she had intended.

He cleared his throat. "That didn't quite come out the way I intended. I realized too late what a wonderful woman I let slip through my fingers. I'd hoped, no prayed, there was another man, a better man than me, you lived happily ever after with…"

An intense emotion shone in Jamie's eyes. Something she'd never witnessed before during any requisite apology he'd made so he could resume his selfish lifestyle. Her swell of anger retreated like a cowboy falling off a rank bull. She believed he meant it. He was sorry for what happened on that long ago night.

Her heart teetered like a leaf stuck to a barb on a fence line. He wanted forgiveness, and she needed to forgive him, yet the strength of her memories reinforced her decision. She couldn't say "I forgive you." Instead she reached out. Awkwardly, she patted his shoulder.

"Thank you, but there wasn't. And, I played a larger part in that choice than you did."

It was true. He'd hurt her, but she'd let the pain consume her heart. It was easier to live with the hurt than open her heart to another man.

A little moisture pooled in her eyes when she gave Jamie a halfhearted shrug. He might have hurt her, causing her to think twice about another relationship. But the choice to not commit fell on her shoulders.

Her pulse pounded in her ears. She wanted to ask him the same question. She parted her lips. Fear outweighed her curiosity. Reconsidering whether she really wanted to know, she turned and walked toward the campground entrance. The swish of her jeans counted off her brisk steps. She hoped Jamie would stay behind. He didn't. His boot heels clicked quickly on the asphalt until he fell into step with her.

Swallowing hard, she stopped and looked directly into his eyes. "Why didn't you marry?" Fear shook her voice.

"You won't like my answer." He gave his head a slight shake, never breaking eye contact.

She put a hand on her hip. "Try me."

Jamie's gaze searched her face, then darted to the ground. He slipped his hands into his front pockets.

The slow lift of his head quickened her heart. The pounding in her ears sounded like a herd of galloping horses.

"My past actions might not have shown it, but there is only one woman for me."

Chapter 3

"You."

A momentary second of shock darkened Donna's caramel-colored eyes and deepened the laugh lines at the outer corners. The rapid flutter of her lashes zapped his heart with fear. Was she going to cry?

Trepidation moistened his palms. He ran his hands down the front of his jeans. He yearned to comfort her. Wrap his arms around her in a loving embrace. Would the gesture open the floodgates, or worse, incite her anger?

His hesitation gave Donna time to absorb what he'd said. Her soft features turned to stone. She opened her mouth.

The blaring honk of a horn coming up from behind them startled Jamie, bringing him back to the reality of their surroundings. The heavy chug of an idling diesel engine warned him an approaching vehicle was pulling up alongside them.

"There you are." Grant pushed his cowboy hat to the back of his head and leaned toward the open passenger window. "I stopped by your camper. When you didn't answer, I thought you might be out on your morning walk. Judging by your duds, you're ready to head to Frontier Park. Can I give you a ride? Ma'am, you're welcome, too." He nodded at Donna.

Jamie reached his hand through the window opening. Grant's solid grasp reflected the strength of their friendship. "Great to see you, buddy."

The slight rise of Grant's bushy eyebrows indicated he'd heard the edge in Jamie's voice and knew why his presence was so welcome. "Everything okay?" His tone remained normal while his sky-blue eyes revealed his concern.

"Yeah." Jamie nodded and smiled at Grant, his friend and sponsor. "This is Donna Greene, a friend from the past."

Stepping away from the side of the pickup, Jamie opened his arm to include Donna in their conversation. "Donna, this is my friend Grant Cornell."

She took a hesitant step forward and tilted her head to look through the window opening. "Nice to meet you."

"The pleasure is mine, ma'am." Grant's full moustache curled up with his smile.

The crew cab of Grant's pickup would comfortably accommodate all of them. Jamie opened the passenger door and gestured his palm for Donna to enter.

"Thank you for the offer. I have to pass. Dustin should be here any minute and you two probably have a lot to talk about. Have a great day." Donna gave them a parade wave, turned on her heel and strode away before Jamie could counter her refusal.

"Hop in, we'll catch her."

Jamie slid into the passenger seat. "I'll let her go." His deep sigh echoed through the cab of the pickup.

"Humph. You will not." Grant's blue eyes twinkled with merriment. "And I don't know why you would. She's a fine-looking woman."

"Yes, she is, and time has made her more beautiful." Jamie watched her shapely form grow small as she put distance between them. "We can wait until Dustin picks her up. Pull over to the side. I need to talk to you anyway."

"Did you tell her?" Grant drummed his thumbs against the steering wheel, filling the pickup cab with a bongo beat.

"Depends on what you mean?" Jamie shrugged.

"You know what I mean."

"No. I did ask her to forgive me." The stiff denim of his jeans rustled when he rubbed his damp palm down his leg. "I want her to forgive me because she's seen I've changed. Not because she knows it's a step in my AA program."

Grant steered his truck to the side of the road, put the stick shift into Neutral, and turned in the seat. "What happened? You didn't turn to alcohol, did you?"

The sun glaring on the windshield, bright and hot, caused Jamie to squint, but he managed to keep Donna in his sights. "I wanted to." The breath he'd been holding whooshed out. His shoulders relaxed.

A white dual-wheeled pickup pulled into the entrance and stopped. Donna opened the passenger door, slipped into the seat and disappeared behind the tinted window.

He looked at Grant, who waited patiently. "I didn't."

"That hasn't happened in what, ten years?"

Jamie jutted out his jaw and gave a slight nod.

"You didn't call me. What stopped you?"

"Donna."

"What triggered your thirst for a drink?"

"Donna."

"Ah." Grant turned and shifted into First. "A bane and a blessing."

Pulling his seat belt across his chest, Jamie clicked the metal end into the fastener. "Never thought of it that way." He ran his right hand down the rough denim of his jeans. "It wasn't really Donna who made me want a drink. It was fear."

Grant turned the vehicle onto the street. "Seeing Donna invited out your old insecurities?"

"Yes, and memories."

Companionable silence surrounded the men while Grant concentrated on navigating through traffic on Dell Range Boulevard.

When a direction sign for Frontier Park came into sight, Grant resumed their conversation. "So you apologized?"

"Kind of." Jamie pulled a Cheyenne Frontier Days pass from his pocket and slid it onto the dashboard. "We need to find the vendor's entrance." He scoured the area.

"I see it." Grant eased into a turn lane and scooted the CFD pass to the corner of the driver side window. "What does kind of mean?"

"I apologized for hurting her."

"And the accident?"

Jamie shook his head. "No, and she didn't really forgive me either."

"You know the Greenes' forgiveness is out of your control, all *you* can do is apologize."

"I know. I really want her to forgive me."

"And love you."

"Yeah, that too." Jamie was thankful for his friendship with Grant. He didn't have to deny or explain his feelings about Donna. Grant understood.

"Any idea where I should park?" Grant stopped the vehicle beside the entrance. The gatekeeper checked the parking pass before waving them through.

"It doesn't matter. We can't park near our location anyway." Jamie checked his watch. They were cutting it close. The volunteers should be in the short overall orientation right now.

"There's an open spot." Grant swung wide in order to park his truck between the marked lines. He killed the engine. "Shall we pray, Pastor Martin?" Grant removed his cowboy hat before he clasped his short chubby fingers and bowed his head.

Jamie mirrored Grant's actions. He cleared his throat. "Lord, be with us today. Help us to lead seekers to You. Enable us to minister to believers and bring Your peace into their lives. Bless our volunteers with compassion and understanding. Protect the cowboys, pickup men, stock hands, clowns, the rodeo personnel, fans and the precious animals. Help us grow the outreach for the Fellowship of Christian Cowboys. Amen."

Donna studied the map she'd been given. The Fellowship of Christian Cowboys was housed in a small tent set up in a grassy area behind the Old West Museum. She traced a path with her finger from Volunteer Square past the Indian Village, through Old Frontier Town finally stopping on the short sidewalk connection to the museum. She tapped a tent with a small cross on top. Even though so much had changed in the last twenty years, it wouldn't be hard to find.

The short volunteer orientation covered so much general information, Donna's brain was on overload while she walked to the FCC location. She wasn't certain if she'd retain any of the specific information the Cowboy Church would surely give their volunteers. She didn't realize when she'd signed up that volunteering involved so much.

Perhaps she should take her name off the list. But if she did, what would she to do with the time between the rodeo competitions? Lie around her trailer? Shop? No, she planned to strengthen her relationship with God. Her clean bill of health changed her mind-set and made her see what was really important in life. She'd reprioritized her life and put God on the top of her list, the place He should have been all along.

Of course, she might just feel emotionally overloaded because of Jamie's statement that she was the only girl for him. It'd been hard to concentrate on the volunteer instructions. Good thing they handed out packets with the information they covered in orientation. Since yesterday when Jamie and Blake came over to help her, her thoughts and feelings were tangled and knotted together like unkempt rope.

She smiled. Why was she even worrying about all the volunteer details? God would guide her. With His help, she could handle anything. Donna drew a deep breath and walked through the entrance of the tent housing the Fellowship of Christian Cowboys.

It took a few minutes for her eyes to adjust to the dimness inside. A table was set up by the door where volunteers could sign in. Donna took her place in the short line with men and women of various ages.

Once she was checked in, name tag on and a required packet of information in hand, Donna surveyed the area. Five rows with six folding chairs in a line ran down the center of the tent. She took a seat in the front row of folding chairs facing a podium and a backdrop screen printed with three rugged wooden crosses. Donna's heart warmed at the simple makeshift pulpit.

She turned in her seat and glanced around the room at the array of Western attire. She fit right in with her red kerchief-print blouse, jeans and boots. A few people wore fancier shirts similar to the one Jamie had on this morning. Actually, there was a man with his back to her wearing the exact same shirt Jamie wore this morning, probably a popular style, especially in Cowboy Church.

Donna opened the folder she was handed and started to read the information. A low chuckle drifted from the corner. She frowned. Were those Jamie's rich tones?

Giving her head a small shake, she rolled her eyes at the thought. Jamie wouldn't be caught dead in a house of God. It'd been a long morning. She'd spent too much time with Jamie. Then she'd replayed their conversation in her head when she was alone. She went back to her reading.

Laughter erupted. Her head jerked up. She studied the back of the gentleman with the white embroidered shirt. She wasn't mistaken. It was Jamie. She swallowed hard. What was he doing here? Had he followed her? Would she get no peace until she forgave him?

Old hurt cinched her heart. Without thinking, she closed her folder and started to stand. She needed to leave. She hated reliving the past. The moment her future changed. *Therefore if anyone is in Christ, he is a new creation; the old has gone, the new has come!*

Donna's eyes widened at the recollection of the scripture from her daily devotions. Slowly she sat back down on the folding chair, the metal seat firm and stable—unlike her faith. She felt Christ's strong hold on her heart now, yet she didn't feel new. Her past wasn't gone. He was standing in the corner. And she would never know the fullness of Christ if she couldn't forgive Jamie.

Her shoulders sagged. She promised she'd give him a chance to prove he'd changed and was sincerely repentant of the past. Jamie volunteering in the Cowboy Church was a step in the right direction. He seemed to be winning over the group he was chatting with, which was nothing new. Jamie had charm and knew how to use it.

As if his heart heard her mind calling his name, Jamie turned, and searched the gathering. His gaze roved the seating area, grazing over her, and then his head snapped back.

His eyes found hers and never broke their hold. She lifted her hand in a weak acknowledgment. He welcomed her with a wide smile, turned to his companions, and after a few handshakes headed her way.

"So you're volunteering here? I can't believe it didn't come up in our conversation this morning." Jamie reached for her with outstretched arms.

She started to lean toward him. Her body longed to once again feel his loving embrace. *No!* Her head and heart weren't in sync. Leaning back in her seat, she grasped one of his hands.

His brows puckered for a brief second. He wrapped his warm fingers around her hand and squeezed, dropping his other arm to his side.

"I guess we were too busy talking about the past."

Donna squirmed in her chair. She didn't mean to verbalize her thought.

Jamie rubbed his chin with the thumb and forefinger of his free hand. "I think from this point forward we should concentrate on the present."

A pang of old hurt thumped her heart. Focusing on the present might be easier said than done.

The old has gone. The scripture fragment helped her push the pain from her heart. She'd try to focus on the here and now. Donna nodded and smiled.

"Great. Is this the first time you've been involved with the Fellowship?" The metal chair next to hers clanked and groaned as Jamie sat down.

"Yes, it is. I thought I needed something to do besides sit in the camper when I wasn't watching the rodeo competition, so I volunteered." The warmth of his hand on hers felt comfortable and familiar.

"Well, I'm glad you chose here." Jamie patted the hand he held then released his grip.

"It's a great place to spend time whether you're a volunteer or just need, well, fellowship."

Jamie's face reflected a peaceful happiness, an expression new to Donna.

"What type of volunteer work do you prefer?"

Donna shrugged. "I'll help out wherever I'm needed. What do you do?"

"My shifts are in the prayer room." Jamie pointed to a corner of the tent where a folding partition was set up. "And the evening worship services."

It was her turn to knit her brows. This was an odd volunteer assignment for Jamie. He'd always been comfortable talking to people, but prayer and worship was a change of character. A pleasant change.

"How would you feel about greeting people? It includes handing out brochures and other information about the organization." Jamie's eyes roamed her face for her reaction.

"That sounds great. What if they have questions I can't answer?"

"Find the pastor on duty. A lot of people who are seeking a relationship with God ask questions."

"Have you been volunteering here a long time?"

"I've been involved in the organization about ten years now."

"Oh!" Donna covered her mouth with her hand. Jamie's tenure with the organization shocked her. Her gasp escaped before she could stop it.

Jamie laughed out loud.

"I'm sorry." Donna tried to regain her composure.

"It's okay. I've gotten that type of reaction before. Not for a long time though." Jamie reached over and squeezed her hand. "Really, Donna, it's okay."

Her nervous laughter erupted around them. "I am sorry."

"I know."

The understanding conveyed in Jamie's eyes lifted her heart. She smiled. "I'm glad to know you volunteer at a worthy organization."

"Thank you, it's near and dear to my heart." Jamie placed his hand over his chest.

"Well, look who we have here."

Grant jingled to a halt in front of them. A key ring packed with keys hung from a belt loop. "These are my keys for the compartments in my truck box."

Donna grimaced, caught in the act of wondering.

"I'm a veterinarian. I keep my tools and medicines locked up. I hate that I have to, but you never know these days." A veil of sadness covered his face.

"So true. A doped animal could cost a cowboy, not to mention what it'd do to a stock contractor." Donna drew her brows together.

The rattling chair beside her drew her attention from Grant. Jamie's left leg bounced nervously. His head hung down.

"You all right?" Grant's voice held a funny edge. He shifted his weight so he stood in front of Jamie.

"Yes."

The rasp in Jamie's voice contrasted with his answer.

"So, Donna." Grant spoke to her, keeping his eyes on Jamie. "Are you here to volunteer?"

"Yes, I am."

"What are you going to be doing?"

Donna knitted her brows. "I haven't decided."

Grant's bushy brows pulled together turning into one. "What? Your assignment and schedule are in your folder."

Jamie's head snapped up. "This is her first year. She should be where she's comfortable so she'll come back and volunteer again."

"Hmm…" Aggravation hummed in the back of her throat. Jamie's backpeddling tone, the first sign of the man she knew in the past. He must have known she signed up to help. It couldn't be why he was here. Could it? She opened her folder and pulled the paper with her name printed on it from under the flap. "I've been assigned to play the piano for Cowboy Church." Her shoulders sagged. She didn't bother to hide the disappointment in her voice.

"You play the piano, which is always a hard spot to fill." Jamie's smile faded.

"Don't you want to play at the services?"

Donna caught the funny look Grant shot Jamie and

the reddening skin on Jamie's neck and cheeks. The conversation was beginning to smell like a rank bull.

"Well?" Jamie's question broke her silence.

"No, I mean yes." Donna stopped. She volunteered to fill the mornings or evenings so she didn't have to sit alone in her camper. She did enough of that at home after work. She shrugged. "Yes, I'll play the piano at the church services. I thought I'd be here for a few hours each day not just an hour each evening."

"I'm sure we can adjust your schedule." Grant smiled politely when he slipped the paper from her hand. His smile turned sly when he headed toward the registration table where a laptop and printer sat. "Again."

"Did he say again?" Donna cocked a brow at Jamie. His skin glowed bright and red like the hot end of a branding iron. Something was going on.

Several moments of awkward silence surrounded them before Jamie gave a slight nod of his head. "I saw your name on the volunteer list. We didn't have a pianist, so I changed your assignment. It won't be a problem if you want more volunteer hours."

"No, it won't." Grant jingled to a stop. "We always have no-shows." He handed Donna a crisp sheet of paper still warm from the printer. "We added some greeter hours to your schedule. Not every day, but six out of ten."

"Great." Donna stared at the schedule. Maybe her volunteer hours coincided with Jamie's? Hope pattered her heart. Adding more volunteer hours might not have been a wise move.

"Pastor." An older lady approached them. "I think we're ready to get started with the orientation."

Donna looked up at Grant. "You're a pastor, too?"

Grant gave his head a shake.

Confused Donna drew her brows together. Who was the elderly lady addressing then? She glanced over her left shoulder. No one stood there.

The rattle of metal drew Donna's attention to Jamie. He stood, placing a hand on her shoulder.

"No, I am."

Chapter 4

Donna chuckled at Jamie's teasing until their eyes locked. His hazel eyes beseeched hers. Jamie was serious. His pleading stare bore into her. Shock pushed away her amusement. Flustered, her chuckle sputtered into sounds of disbelief at Jamie's unexpected revelation.

She clamped her lips tight in an effort to check her surprise. Mesmerized by the intense emotion in his eyes, she kept her gaze riveted to his, trying to read his unspoken message. Was he simply trying to gage her reaction or did he want her approval?

Surely he didn't want or need her approval after all these years. Besides if approval was what he sought, she couldn't grant it. She might find it in her heart to forgive him for his past mistakes, but she *knew* the events of his past. He had no business preaching anything to anybody, especially God's word.

This new revelation confirmed her earlier doubts.

She couldn't honor her volunteer hours with the FCC now. She grimaced at the hypocrisy of the situation and dropped her gaze to the packet in her hand. Shouldn't a preacher have always walked the walk and talked the talk? Jamie didn't fit the job description. At all.

Loneliness looped her insides and squeezed. Not honoring her volunteer duties meant she'd spend her time alone in a crowd or passing time in the camper, just like at home. Somehow she'd thought this time away would be different. Disappointment spun through her until she released a deep sigh.

"Donna?"

She drew a shallow breath and started to slowly lift her head.

"Pastor?"

Donna looked at the elderly woman who addressed Jamie. Confusion etched the woman's features.

"Go on." Donna sputtered the command at Jamie and waved him off with her hand.

Jamie leaned toward her. "I want to talk to you about this, and well, many other things." After his whispered words, Jamie swallowed hard. Sadness replaced the pleading in his eyes. He gave her a weak smile and turned to follow the older woman.

"He's not the man you once knew."

Donna turned her attention to Grant and shrugged her response. She was speechless. The party boy she'd fallen in love with twenty years ago never stepped foot in a church. He'd had no time for organized religion or anything that made him feel guilty about his actions. It was hard to believe he'd had a change of heart. A big change of heart.

Knowing how Jamie felt about God in the past, she couldn't in good conscience volunteer here. She straightened the packet of papers on her lap and reached for her purse resting on the floor. She stood and swung the strap over her shoulder. She pushed the sheet of paper with her volunteer schedule toward Grant. "I'm sorry…"

"Don't do this. Stay and give him a chance. It'd mean a lot to him."

Why exactly did Grant think she'd care about Jamie's feelings? Irritation swirled through her. After what Jamie had done to her and her family twenty years ago, he was the last person who should be standing behind a pulpit.

The sheet of paper rustled as she wiggled her wrist trying to get Grant to take back the schedule. Grant kept his hands stuffed in the front pockets of his blue jeans. It was no use, Grant supported Jamie. Pursing her lips, she turned to lay the sheet of paper on the seat of a folding chair.

She lifted her eyes and realized fifteen to twenty people were waiting to hear Jamie's welcome speech. A few of their eyes darted her way. Others looked down or away in avoidance. Lost in the moment, she'd forgotten where she was. Why had she chosen to sit in the front row? Was it too late to make a graceful escape?

Flustered, she glanced around. It was.

Jamie's voice boomed through a microphone. "Good morning. Please everyone take a seat."

Looking out over the crowd, Jamie's smile was broad and welcoming until his gaze settled on her. His confident smile faded. She interpreted his slight nod toward the chair as an unspoken plea.

A flush crept up her cheeks. Never again would she choose to sit in the front row. She slid down on the chair next to her volunteer list. Grant took a seat two chairs down.

By now the low chatter of the crowd hushed. Jamie smiled at her and she lowered her eyes, hoping he picked up on her cue. She didn't want to be here listening to him preach the word of the Lord.

"Let's open with prayer."

Donna lowered her head and folded her hands. She'd use the time to seek the Lord's guidance in this difficult situation. *Dear God...* Her prayer came to an abrupt stop when Jamie began his.

Instead of his low booming announcer voice, Jamie's baritone was soft and earnest. His tone comforted and reassured. It made her want to lift her head to be sure it was Jamie who spoke. Putting her prayer on hold, she listened intently to the words of his petition. Perhaps she'd catch one higher octave or hear his voice crack. Anything that might give away his real feelings about God. It never came. Jamie's tone remained sincere, his prayer heartfelt.

She lifted her head on the *Amen*. Although Jamie's stance was confident, it wasn't cocky. When he raised his chin, he looked her way. His gaze roamed her face before his hazel eyes locked to hers. A shiver quivered through her at the peace shining from his eyes.

Donna drew her brows together at the unexpected feeling.

Therefore if anyone is in Christ, he is a new creation; the old has gone, the new has come!

Cocking her head to the side, Donna crossed her arms over her chest. Since her recovery, she tried to listen to God's nudging. Was she being too judgmental of Jamie? Allowing the scorned feelings of a young girl to fog her thoughts? Jamie really did seem different. He wanted to make amends. His words and actions held a high level of sincerity.

A year ago she had wanted to seek him out and make amends. What better venue than this to spend time with Jamie? They'd be surrounded by people. She knew him well enough to pick up on any nuances from the past. She'd know then if he had changed or he'd just improved his skill at charming people.

Donna glanced at her volunteer schedule. In a quick motion, she slid the paper from the metal seat and stuffed it in the packet. She wasn't off to a good start. She'd been so lost in thought, she'd missed most of the information Jamie relayed to the volunteers. She'd have to talk to Jamie one-on-one to find out the expectations for the volunteers. Although she hated to admit to Jamie that she hadn't been paying attention, she would. She planned to assess Jamie's behavior while she honored her volunteer hours.

Jamie stood at the end of the camp spot between the two trailers, holding a full coffee carafe. He knew Donna was in her camper. He knew she was alone. He knew he needed to see her and explain.

Shifting his weight from one foot to the other, he tried to get his courage up to go knock on her door. Maybe she didn't even drink coffee anymore.

"Uncle Jamie, what are you doing?"

Blake's voice startled Jamie. "Shush, you don't have to holler."

Gravel crunched under Blake's feet. "I'm not hollering. This is my normal voice."

In the faint last light of dusk, Jamie caught Blake's eye-roll.

"I'm meeting a few guys in town. We're going to check out the Frontier Days activities. Want to come?"

Jamie licked his lips. It'd be easier to go get reacquainted with his vice than rekindle Donna's friendship. He gave his head a shake. "I'll hang around the RV park."

Out of the corner of his eye, Jamie saw movement by one of Donna's camper windows. The curtain corner had been moved to the side and Donna's silhouette shaded the screen.

"It's only us, Jamie and Blake." Jamie didn't want Donna to be frightened since she was staying alone. Sometimes partiers knocked on the wrong camper door.

"I can see who it is. What are you two doing?"

"I'm going into town." Blake tipped his hat in the direction of the window. "I have no idea what Uncle Jamie is doing."

Jamie's heart thundered in his chest.

"He's got coffee though, so maybe you'll have a cup with him so I can get on my way?" Blake planted his straw cowboy hat on his head, leaned close to Jamie and snickered. "Thought you needed a little help," Blake whispered. He turned on his heel and walked off. "Don't wait up."

Jamie's emotions turned into a full-fledged storm. His thundering heart resounded in his ears. Fear and anxiety, ragged and sharp, crackled through him like lightning bolts cut through dark, threatening clouds.

The click of Blake's boot heels against the blacktop, the ping of the pickup door opening and closing and the roar of the diesel engine filled the silence hanging between Jamie and Donna's open window.

Donna pressed her face closer to the screen. Jamie could make out the outline of her nose and chin.

"I brought the coffee if you have the cups?" He lifted the carafe in the air until it was even with his head.

"That is, if you'd care for a cup of coffee and some company." Jamie's words came quick as if he was backpedaling out of a bad date.

He cleared his throat. "What I mean is…"

"I know what you mean. I'll be out in a minute with cups. There are two lawn chairs leaning against the front of the camper."

Jamie rested the carafe on the ground and unfolded the fabric woven chairs. He placed them what he considered companionably close.

The dim light of a lamp in Donna's camper cut through the darkness as she opened the door and stepped out. She'd changed into comfortable athletic clothes. Light blue jersey pants hit below her knee. A loose oversized T-shirt was screen printed with butterflies across her chest. The vibrant blue, purple and orange of the butterflies grew brighter in the darkness when she closed the door. Her outfit struck Jamie. Over the years he'd pictured her still wearing Western-cut shirts and denim jeans that fit like a second skin.

Jamie looked down at his own clothes. His cargo shorts, T-shirt and athletic shoes were a far cry from how he dressed in his youth, too.

She carefully stepped down the thin camper step in her flip-flops. Two coffee cups dangled precariously from her fingers looped through the handles. "That nephew of yours is a little dickens."

Her soft chuckle took the edge off Jamie's nerves.

"That he is. I'm sorry if he put you on the spot." Jamie raised his palms. "Don't feel you have to…"

"I don't." Donna's direct answer wasn't curt or commanding and helped put Jamie at ease. "Do you think we need some light? I have a camping lantern."

"No, you'll be okay once your eyes adjust to the

darkness." Jamie motioned for Donna to take a seat. "Besides, your shirt is creating light of its own."

Donna pulled on the hem of the T-shirt with one hand and looked down at the design. "It was a gift from my nieces." She grimaced and lifted a hand to her chest and rubbed across the butterflies in flight.

Jamie hadn't meant his comment as criticism. "I didn't mean anything bad. Your shirt is nice." The style and colors suited her.

"What?" Donna looked up at him.

"I said I like the glow-in-the-dark butterflies on your shirt. Your nieces have good taste." Jamie fought the urge to roll his eyes at his own lame statement. This shouldn't be so hard. He felt as if he was back in high school groping for something to say to a pretty girl. At least his tongue hadn't grown thick. He and Donna should be past this awkward stage. Jamie's heart sagged. Their stilted relationship was his fault.

"Thank you. Let's have a seat." Donna walked over to the lawn chairs.

Once they were seated, Jamie reached down and lifted the thermal container and poured coffee into the cups Donna held. Donna handed him a cup after he sat the coffee carafe on the ground between their chairs.

While Donna took a sip, Jamie took the opportunity to be the first one to speak.

"You hurried off this morning. I was hoping to talk to you." Jamie gripped the coffee mug with both hands. Focusing his attention on the heat seeping through the thin ceramic of the cup warming his palms, he waited for Donna's response.

"Dustin was waiting to give me a ride back here and I needed a little time to adjust to…" Donna paused and turned in her chair. "You. Or the change in you."

Donna was never one to mince words. None of the Greenes had a problem with speaking their minds. They were direct shooters. A trait Jamie admired. Tonight, with his nerves jittering from the conversation he needed to have with Donna, he was glad for the cloak of darkness. Although he knew everyone was vulnerable, he wanted, no needed, Donna to view him as strong.

"I should have told you my other occupation this morning. I became a lay minister about eight years ago."

Even in the darkness, Jamie felt the scrutiny of Donna's intense stare. She lifted her cup to her lips again, never taking her eyes off him. The white strands in her chestnut hair glistened in the moonlight.

Jamie followed her lead. A large part of him wished his swig of coffee held the bitter flavor of an Irish coffee. He managed to tamp down the longing for a taste of alcohol to a faint reminder most days. When he faced difficult situations, the urge raged strong, trying to take control of him.

"You took me by surprise. It's not an occupation I'd ever have guessed you'd try."

"I know. For a long time I questioned God's existence. I'm ashamed to say I didn't really believe He did exist." Jamie sat his full cup on the ground. The coffee wasn't helping quell his nerves or his thirst for a drink.

Donna shifted in her seat. "What changed?"

She'd given him the opening he needed. A chance to explain everything, even the reason he wanted her forgiveness.

"I met Grant. He took me to a meeting where other men and women depended upon God to get them through each day." The memory of the first Alcoholics Anonymous meeting Jamie attended quickened his breathing. Although he'd told Grant he thought he had a drinking problem, it was the first time he admitted his dependence publically. The words about choked him before he got them out. Over the years those few words grew easier and easier to say. Until tonight. The same fear clogged his throat.

"Was it a church meeting?" Donna drained her cup.

Jamie shook his head. "No, it wasn't." He sucked in a breath of cool night air and let his words rush from him. "My name is Jamie and I'm an alcoholic."

Time seemed to stop while he waited for Donna's reaction.

The darkness didn't cover her shock. Eyes wide-open, jaw dropped. Her lips started to move, then stopped. She drew a deep breath and with its release her features softened. Her eyelashes fluttered and a sad smile crept to her lips. She reached out and covered his hand, which had a death grip on the lawn chair's armrest, with hers. "I'm sorry it came to that for you."

Jamie wasn't after sympathy. He needed forgiveness. Swallowing hard he hoped to remove the lump in his throat and the longing to taste alcohol from the tip of his tongue. It didn't work, but he knew he needed to continue. Donna was open and actually listening.

"After the accident and the aftermath…"

Donna's gaze dropped. She seemed suddenly interested in the bottom of her coffee cup.

"My partying spun out of control. The first thing I did in the morning was take a drink. The last thing I did at night was take a drink. It's the only way I could live with myself over what I'd done to your family. To you."

Sliding down in her lawn chair, Donna rested her head on the metal edge, looking up at the star-filled sky before turning her head his way.

Her attention gave him the courage to continue. "I found God at those meetings. Other alcoholics spoke of how He worked in their lives, turning around relationships, giving them a future. Their faith intrigued me. I started attending church and Bible study. When I felt weak, I'd read Bible passages. God's word has helped me stay sober for the past ten years. Sharing His teachings with others is a small repayment for all God's done for me."

"Amen, Pastor Martin."

Jamie placed his free hand over Donna's. She didn't try to pull her hand away. "Grant said you picked up your volunteer schedule. Will I be seeing you around the Fellowship of Christian Cowboys?"

"Yes." Donna turned her head and gazed upward.

Mirroring her posture, Jamie laced his fingers through hers and stared up into the stars. His thirst had been quenched. He should be continuing with his conversation, asking for her forgiveness. There would be time to discuss that later. Right now, he was doing what they'd taught him in AA, taking one day at a time and living in the moment—a very enjoyable moment.

Chapter 5

"I'm telling you, it doesn't make any sense to have Dustin drive out to the campground to pick you up when you can ride to Frontier Park with Blake and me." Hands on his hips, Jamie stood in front of her open camper door, his tone edged with aggravation.

She should never have held hands with him under the starry Wyoming sky. She'd sent the wrong message. She didn't want to start a relationship. She'd given in to a weak moment, knowing they had both faced trouble over the years. Alone. Her family and friends had been supportive, the same way she suspected Grant had been there for Jamie, but it wasn't the same. She'd witnessed husband-and-wife intimacy over the years with her parents' and siblings' marriages. The intuitiveness of knowing what someone needs before they ask. Understanding another person's limitations. Loving someone more than yourself.

The way she'd loved Jamie once. A small part of her heart still belonged to Jamie and loved him unconditionally. It was the reason she'd tried to comfort him last night. A small thread of hope wound around her heart, urging her to forgive his past transgressions and perhaps start over.

With the bright morning came the realization that Jamie was no longer the man she once knew, and most of the girl he fell in love with didn't exist either. Time and life experience had changed them. They'd never recapture their youthful passion.

When her brother, Cameron, called to see if she'd settled in, she felt so guilty about spending time with Jamie she could barely carry on a conversation with him. If he knew Jamie was her campsite neighbor, he'd come unglued.

Even though Jamie made an excellent point and looked handsome today in a light blue short-sleeved Western-cut shirt and faded denim jeans, she needed to keep her resolve. "He doesn't mind."

"I didn't say he did mind." Jamie flopped his hands in the air. "I said, with the price of gas and since we're heading into town anyway, it doesn't make any sense. Besides, if he doesn't get here pretty soon, he'll be late for his event."

No kidding. Donna checked her watch.

"And so will Blake." Jamie hitched a thumb toward his nephew.

"Really, ma'am."

Donna raised her brows at Blake.

"I mean, Donna." Dimples formed in his cheeks when he smiled at her. "It's no trouble. We have plenty of room in the pickup. I do need to get a move on though."

Blake was harder to resist than his uncle. She couldn't think of one rebuttal as to why she shouldn't ride over to Frontier Park with them. Besides, Dustin was supposed to be here twenty minutes ago. Knowing how her nephew liked the ladies, he'd probably lost track of time talking to a pretty girl at the pancake breakfast.

"Okay, give me a second to call Dustin and grab my purse."

She'd been right. Dustin was still downtown. He apologized for losing track of time and said he'd be right over. She heard the relief in his voice when she told him she'd found other transportation. Sticking her cell phone in her purse, she walked to the bedroom and gave herself a once-over in the mirror. Suddenly, she wasn't certain about the outfit she'd chosen, a knee-skimming dark denim skirt, white cotton blouse and red cowboy boots. She'd accessorized with a patriotic-colored necklace-and-earrings set in honor of Military Day. Maybe she should change.

The purr of a truck engine outside of her window changed her mind. Anyway, she reminded herself, this was only Jamie. Running her fingers through her hair, she donned her straw cowboy hat, grabbed her purse from the counter and locked her door.

Jamie stood with the truck door open and assisted her into the pickup. He and Blake both honored Military Day with their choice of shirts in red, white and blue.

Traffic was light and so was the conversation. When they reached the wrought-iron entrance gate of Frontier Park, Blake eased the pickup to a stop. "Mind if I let you two out here? I need to get my horse ready for today's event." Blake drummed his thumbs on the steering wheel to the beat of the country love song playing on the radio.

"It's fine with me. Jamie, if you want to go with Blake, I'm fine on my own. I need to pick up my tickets for today's rodeo performance." Donna slid from the backseat of the crew cab pickup and secured her purse on her shoulder.

"I do, too. We can walk together." Jamie slammed the pickup door shut and waved Blake off.

Donna glanced around the area. So much had changed since the last time she'd attended a rodeo in Cheyenne. She had no idea where she needed to go so she let Jamie take the lead.

They entered Frontier Park. Jamie turned to his left opposite the Indian Village and cut through the parking lot. They passed sponsor booths on their way to the ticket office.

The brick ticket office came into view. Jamie led them to the end of the short line. The midmorning sun warmed Donna's shoulders.

"You don't mind company at the rodeo, do you?" Jamie turned to face her. The mirrored lenses of his sunglasses caught the sun's glare. Her reflection made her feel as if she was talking to herself even though she tried to see his eyes.

She hadn't quite thought this part through. Conversing with Jamie around the campers or the Fellowship of Christian Cowboys was one thing; being seen together on the rodeo grounds was another. Cameron would be on the grounds. He'd spend most his time in the livestock area, but there was a chance he could see them. Dread dipped her heart. She didn't want to listen to a lecture from her older brother.

Her mouth drew up in a tight smile. She glanced over both shoulders. "If you have your ticket, don't worry about me." Donna pulled her hand free of Jamie's. It only took an instant for her to miss his touch. "And I'm sure I can get a ride back to the campsite from Dustin. *Or Cameron*." With those sunglasses covering Jamie's most expressive feature, it was hard to read his face.

"I don't have my ticket yet. We might as well sit together."

They chose their seats and paid. Jamie placed his hand on the small of her back and guided her to the entrance gate. The short line moved quickly. Donna's purse was small enough it didn't necessitate her having to open it to be searched.

The area opened up to exhibit halls filled with merchandise booths, the carnival, grandstand and food vendors. Sweet and tangy aromas mingled together promising patrons a mouthwatering treat. "Would you care for something to eat?"

"I think so. Something light though. I plan to eat popcorn while I watch the rodeo performance." Donna pointed to a sign on a carnival food wagon. "I'm going to try a taco in a bag."

"Sounds good to me."

Jamie ordered for both of them. Donna fished a ten-dollar bill from her purse, and Jamie pushed it back at her.

"My treat." Jamie slipped his sunglasses off, folded the temples and stuck them in his shirt pocket.

"I can't let you do that." Donna pushed the bill toward Jamie, who looked down at it and back up at Donna. The sun caught the green flecks in Jamie's hazel eyes, making them sparkle like emeralds.

"You can buy next time."

Next time? Donna drew a deep breath. He had gotten the wrong idea last night. She needed to set him straight.

Jamie handed her two snack-sized corn chips bags

opened at the top and filled with taco meat, tomatoes, cheese and lettuce. The vendor had tucked plastic forks down the sides. Jamie carried their drinks to a picnic table. Once he set their drinks down, he took a chips bag from Donna and assisted her while she slipped onto the bench. He slid onto the opposite bench and forked a bite. "This is good." He nodded.

"And different." Donna took another bite of her lunch.

They ate in silence. Donna wiped her mouth and stuffed the paper napkin into the bag and began to sip her homemade lemonade.

Jamie held out his hand for her garbage, walked to a nearby trash can, and pitched it in. When he returned he snagged his drink from the table.

Before Donna knew it, Jamie had hold of her hand and was leading her through the throngs of people in the walkway. Jamie zigzagged through the crowd and entered a portal under the grandstand.

"Pastor Martin, Pastor Martin."

He stopped at a vendor booth and stuck out his hand in welcome. "Donna, this is Gus Hardin. He makes the finest custom ropes you'll ever find."

"Pastor Martin, you are too kind."

"Gus, this is Donna Greene."

"Very nice to meet you. Are you part of the stock contractor's family?" Gus smiled wide in Donna's direction.

"Yes, he's my brother. I'm here to watch my nephew Dustin Bliss compete in the tie-down roping event."

"Dustin Bliss? He's having as good of a year as Blake. I don't know." Gus's eyes twinkled. He waggled a finger in warning. "You two should not be cavorting together with Jamie's nephew also in contention."

A flush started to creep up Donna's neck at Gus's reference. She loosened her grip on Jamie's hand. Jamie held tight to her hand and flashed her a smile.

A young woman sprinted to Gus's side before he could tease them anymore. "Did I hear you say something about the top tie-down ropers?"

Gus sighed deeply. "This is my daughter, Brittney. She just graduated college with a business degree and thinks I need to expand my business."

"Daddy." Brittney rolled her eyes and shook hands with Donna and Jamie. "If your nephews need a new rope, send them our way."

"We will. We'd better get going, we need to find our seats. It was nice to see you, Gus, and nice to meet you, Brittney." Jamie slipped on his mirrored aviator sunglasses and pulled Donna back into the main corridor of people.

"You, too, Pastor Martin."

Donna shook her head. It sounded so strange to hear Jamie called Pastor Martin. It also seemed strange that people genuinely liked to see Jamie. In his younger years, his boasting and cocky attitude turned off many people. She'd witnessed more than one person avoid Jamie or make an excuse to not have to talk to him.

When those situations had happened, it always irritated her since love had clouded her eyes to most of Jamie's faults. She hadn't understood then how people could act that way. Once you got past the veneer of Jamie's bravado, he was a decent person. It appeared people were able to see the real Jamie now. Then again, she'd only caught one brief glimpse of the old Jamie.

"You'd better get the popcorn now before we climb up to our seats. I'd hate to have you go up and then all the way back down just to pay me back for lunch." Jamie's lips quirked into a smile. Donna didn't need to see his hazel eyes to know they sparkled like sequins on a rodeo queen's gown.

"How nice of you to take pity on me." She quirked a brow and placed her hand on a hip to emphasize her sarcasm.

"I do what I can." Jamie gave her a lighthearted smile, which she returned.

Donna fished through her purse to get her wallet ready and stepped into the concession line. It was a large rodeo. What were the odds of running into Cameron? Or Cameron spotting them in the crowd? Besides, she was having a good time this morning, and sitting with Jamie beat watching the noonday performance alone.

It seemed to Jamie he stole a glance to his left every second to make sure Donna still sat by his side. Which was silly. He knew she was there, he smelled her flowery perfume. She'd made good on her promise and purchased a large popcorn for them to share. They'd both chosen water to drink instead of soda.

They discussed everything happening in the arena. When a feisty black stallion kicked up a fuss in the stall, Donna turned to him.

"That's Buckaroo. He's going to the National Finals."

Jamie's heart galloped in his chest and his mouth went dry. He'd been so happy to have Donna by his side, maybe in his life again, he'd forgotten her brother contracted the stock for the rodeo.

Pride shined from Donna's face as she watched the hands calm Buckaroo down in order for the cowboy to mount his back. All stock contractors dreamed of having their animals selected for the Super Bowl of rodeo. Twenty years ago, the Greene family pinned their hopes on a bull. It would have been the first time their stock made the grade for the National Finals.

Sweat trickled down the side of his face even though the memory made his blood run cold. Jamie felt Donna's eyes move from the action in the chute to him, searching for a response no doubt.

He drew a deep breath and rubbed his palms down the crease in his jeans before turning to Donna. Her eyes roved his face. When her eyes grew wide, her smile faded.

The chink of the chute flying open drew her attention away from him. By the roar of the crowd, Buckaroo lived up to his reputation and threw the cowboy. Jamie looked over in time to see the cowboy jump up and run for the fence.

When the announcer asked the crowd to clap for the cowboy because it was the only pay he'd get today, Jamie and Donna obliged.

A trick rider flew past the length of the grandstand demonstrating the suicide drag to entertain the crowd while the hands prepared for the next event, tie-down roping.

"Congratulations." Jamie barely heard his words over his heartbeat drumming in his ears. He didn't want to talk about the Greenes' rodeo stock yet he couldn't ignore her comment. "I know what it means to a stock contractor to have their animals chosen for the National Finals."

Donna shrugged. "Thanks."

Jamie lowered his sunglasses and searched her face. "I am so sorry for what I did to your family's business and you."

Donna nodded her head. "I believe you."

"Do you forgive me?"

Sadness veiled Donna's eyes. She released a sigh. "I don't know." She gave him a weak smile. "Let's concentrate on our nephews and not our past today. All right?"

Nodding, Jamie slipped his sunglass back up his nose.

The announcer's voice boomed through the loud-speakers.

"This guy, Grady Hawthorne, is gaining in points on Blake. Dustin too. His hands fly when he's tying his half hitch."

"It's where he gains his time?" Donna stretched her body trying to get a good look at the cowboy backing his horse into the chute.

Jamie rubbed his chin and leaned close to Donna. "I don't think so. His horse is really fast coming out of the chute yet he never breaks the barrier."

Donna leaned closer to Jamie's ear. "Some horses are fast."

"I know." Jamie held his hands up. "But watch."

The cowboy gave a nod. The gate flew open. The horse lurched once and was at a full gallop chasing a brown-and-white-spotted calf with a thirty-foot head start. The cowboy's lasso found its mark. He was off his horse trailing a gloved hand down the rope while the horse backed up, keeping the rope taut. In seconds, the cowboy threw the calf down, dropped to his knees, worked magic with his rope and threw his hands in the air.

The announcer waited for the time keeper's report. "Ten seconds flat. Grady Hawthorne has set the bar high today."

Donna fisted her hands and snorted in excitement. "His horse and his hands are fast. I hope our boys have a good day."

Surprised looped through Jamie and tied his heart in a half hitch. Donna was such a loving person, she didn't just want Dustin to succeed. She wanted good things for Blake, too. "We'll know in a minute."

Jamie jerked his head toward the chute. Dustin aligned his dappled mare into the small corner of the chute. After a few rope adjustments, Dustin gave a nod and the race was on. A black calf launched from the pen and made it a quarter of the way down the arena before the loop of Dustin's rope dropped over it. With practiced accuracy, Dustin was off his horse, had flanked his calf, hit his knees and laced a rope around both of the calf's hind legs and one front leg. The timer above the chutes stopped when he threw his hands in the air.

"He made good time." Jamie looked at Donna who was holding her breath. She reached over and squeezed his hand.

"I know." Donna's voice held excitement and awe.

After the required time passed to ensure the calf stayed roped, the announcer's voice echoed through the arena. "Oh, boy, we've got a nine point two five folks. Dustin Bliss has taken the lead."

"I hope Blake does as well." Donna put her pinkies in her mouth and blew a shrill whistle.

"I hope so, too. There's a few riders before him." Jamie knew the first two cowboys' times would throw Blake's confidence. He removed his Stetson. *Lord, please keep Blake calm and confident. Remind him this is a talent You provided and the fact that he is using this talent is more important than where he places in the competition. Amen.*

Running a hand through his hair, he set the hat back on his head. Six ropers took their turns. Two broke the barriers, adding penalty points to their already high times and knocking them out of contention. Three chased their calves down the full length of the arena without their rope even making contact with the calf. One roped his calf right out of the gate, but had trouble getting its legs aligned and lost some time, finishing with a sixteen.

When Blake took his position, it was Jamie's turn to hold his breath. Blake appeared confident. Too bad it hadn't rubbed off on his horse. The chestnut quarter horse danced on its back legs and spun in a small circle in the chute. Blake rode him out and turned him around, trying to get into place. It didn't work and he tried again. This time the horse seemed to settle down.

Rope in hand, Blake gave a nod. The chute clanked open. Jamie began to call the play of the event in his mind as if he were behind the microphone. *The cowboy is out of the gate with his lariat spinning. This horse is trained. Look how it takes the cowboy right to the calf's side. The loop is in the air and found its target. Blake is off his horse and trailing down the rope. See how his horse helps him by pulling on the rope, keeping it tight. One leg, two legs, three legs and a half hitch. The cowboy's hands are in the air. It's going to be a good time.*

His last call snapped him out of his reverie. He looked at the digital timer and breathed out his relief.

"Nine point three five seconds." The announcer shouted. "Blake Martin takes second place."

The same shrill whistle sounded to his left. Donna was on her feet.

Standing, Jamie clapped his hands and whooped. He turned to Donna. She reached out her arms. He grabbed her, wrapping her in a hug. Her arms tightened around him. The years and noise faded. He was home. The comfort of Donna's arms was his balm against the world. Her hold loosened. Jamie caught her arms before they fell to her side, trailing his hands down her soft skin. He held her at arm's-length, staring intently into her eyes.

Those beautiful caramel-brown eyes emitted more than happiness over their nephews' scores. Was it love? Were her old feelings returning, too? She leaned toward him and her eyelids flickered shut. He dipped his head. Just as his lips brushed hers the loudspeakers crackled.

"Cameron Greene report to pen number three."

Donna's eyes flew open. She stared wide-eyed at Jamie before she stiffened and pushed out of his embrace. The color and happiness drained from her face. Fear and sadness erased the gleam from her eyes.

"Sorry for the public service announcement." The announcer joked with the crowd. "There's a rank bull acting up back there, folks. Cameron Greene, can you hear me? They need you in pen number three."

Jamie looked at Donna. She'd dropped to the bleacher and sat ramrod straight with her hands clamped between her knees. Her eyes focused straight ahead on something in the arena.

"Sorry about that, folks." The announcer boomed.

He couldn't be sorrier than Jamie.

Chapter 6

"Looked for you at the rodeo this afternoon. I was sure we had seats together." Grant's forehead wrinkled with the lift of his bushy eyebrows. "Guess I must have been wrong." He fished a ticket stub from his pocket and studied it.

"You're not wrong and you know it." Jamie snapped out the words, taking out his frustration about the abrupt turn his enjoyable afternoon had taken on Grant. He wiped his lips with the back of his hand, an old habit of his that used to follow a long swig of beer.

"Stop thinking about taking a drink right now." Grant pointed a finger his way. "Let's talk about what happened."

Grant dragged two of the folding chairs toward the prayer room corner of the Cowboy Church to give them privacy. The chair legs vibrated over the bumpy ground causing the seats to clack against the metal legs. The noise grated on Jamie's nerves. He winced, tensing his shoulders even more. "Give me one of those." Jamie grabbed a chair from Grant and carried it to the canvas wall.

Placing the chair facing the tent side, Jamie threw his leg over the seat and sat on the chair backward, resting his arms on the cool metal edge.

"So?" Grant faced his chair inches from Jamie. The metal hinges groaned under his weight when he dropped onto the seat. "Blake told me you browbeat Donna into riding to Frontier Park with you."

"I didn't browbeat her. It didn't make any sense for Dustin." Jamie stopped when he saw Grant's satisfied grin. "Okay, you got me. I wanted to spend time with Donna. When I found out she didn't have a ticket to the rodeo…"

"You decided to blow me off and buy another ticket?"

Jamie rubbed his thumb across the stubble on his chin. "Yeah, I guess so. I didn't think she should sit alone."

"How did she feel about it?"

"She seemed okay with it. We had a quick lunch. Things started feeling comfortable between us again."

"Then why are you acting like such a sore loser. Blake had a good turnout today. You enjoyed the performance with a pretty woman by your side."

"Because maybe we became too comfortable." Jamie shrugged.

Grant eye's widened. "What do you mean?"

"Well, we were both cheering for Blake and Dustin. After Blake's run, when we found out they were in the top three, we, well, we celebrated with a hug."

"Jamie, any man would be happy, on top of the world, if a pretty woman hugged him." Grant threw his hands in the air in mock aggravation drawing a grin from Jamie.

"I know and I was elated. So was Donna. When the hug ended and we looked into each other's eyes, she leaned toward me. Our lips brushed and I planned to kiss her when the announcer paged Cameron and Donna froze. The rest of the afternoon she reverted back to one- or two-word answers. Right after the bull riding event ended, she pulled out her cell phone and called Dustin, asking for a ride back to RV park."

"Tough break." Grant clapped him on the biceps, vibrating his shoulders. "Maybe you should try reeling in your emotions and work on the forgiveness aspect of this relationship first."

"Easier said than done." Jamie closed his eyes. Donna touched his heart in places no one else could.

"Are you doing okay otherwise?"

Jamie opened his eyes to Grant's concerned stare. "I am, although the urge to take a drink has been stronger since I arrived and found out Donna was my park neighbor. The accident seems fresh again, like it happened yesterday. If only I could remember more about that night."

"Excuse me."

A petite blonde, about nineteen, stood beside Jamie's chair. "Which one of you is the pastor on duty? The lady over there pointed me in this direction."

Throwing his leg over the chair, Jamie stood. Grant nodded a silent greeting as he eased from his chair and crossed the room. Jamie assessed the young woman's body language. She crossed her arms and hugged her body. Lonely and scared? "I'm Pastor Martin." He tipped his hat rather than extending his hand since her stance was wary.

"Afton Taylor." She managed a smile. "I really need to talk to someone."

"Have a seat. You've come to the right place."

Donna slid into the cab of Cameron's pickup. The fatigue of her restless night pressed heavy on her shoulders and eyelids. She rested her forehead against the glass of the passenger window and closed her eyes giving them the repose she should have last night.

Although she had tried not to, Donna kept an eye on Jamie and Blake's camper until the wee hours of the morning. Each time she awoke, which was often, she peeked out the camper window. She never did see a light on, however when Cameron drove past this morning, the pickup was parked close to the door.

She'd had the silly notion Jamie might bring coffee over again last night so they could sit under the stars together. Why she thought Jamie would come calling after she froze at the rodeo, she didn't know.

Donna gingerly fingered her mouth. Tingles of the brush of Jamie's lips lingered there. The crack of love's electricity woke up her heart the same way it had twenty years ago. She didn't push all of her other suitors away to avoid being hurt. The truth was, a relationship didn't develop with any of them because their touch didn't light her up inside the way Jamie's did.

"Are you sure you don't want to go to the parade?"

Shaking her head, she turned to her brother. "It'd be nice to go to the parade, but I have volunteer hours at the FCC."

Cameron gave her a narrow-eyed stare. "You look different today. And you smell really nice."

A rush of panic caused her to catch her breath. She smoothed her palms down the soft denim of her skirt.

Her jersey shirt with a silver studded design around the neckline matched her red cowboy boots. She hadn't accentuated her femininity in a long time. Jamie brought out her desire to be womanly. Had she overdone it? Given herself away? "It's probably because I'm tired. I didn't sleep well last night. I thought a little perfume might perk me up." She managed to keep her tone even.

"Were your neighbors partying all night, keeping you awake?"

"No, not at all." Donna turned her head and looked out the passenger window. She hadn't lied to her brother, yet she felt like she had. His hatred for Jamie had never died. If he knew Jamie and Blake were her neighbors in the campground...

"I know Jamie Martin and his nephew Blake are camped beside you."

Donna's head jerked involuntarily. Had she voiced her thoughts out loud? Jamie had been front and center in her thoughts since yesterday afternoon's rodeo performance. Her lips formed the word *how* but her fear silenced her voice.

Cameron answered her unspoken question. "Dustin told me."

Irritated, Donna drummed her fingers on the window ledge. At forty-four, she didn't need the male population of the Greene family standing guard over her.

"Have you seen him?"

"Yes." Donna stared straight ahead, squinting at the sun's glare through the windshield.

"And?"

The silence in the cab of the pickup grew thick and heavy.

"Are you going to answer me?"

The big brother I-know-what's-best-for-you-tone flared Donna's temper. "I did answer you. I told you I've seen him."

"And?"

"There is no and." Donna's fingers picked up pace, drumming to the same tempo as her thundering heart. She was conflicted enough with her and Jamie's whisper of a kiss. The last thing she needed today was to deal with her grudge-holding sibling.

"I heard there was dinner."

Dustin was going to get a talking-to the next time Donna saw him.

"I also know he's involved in Cowboy Church." Cameron clipped out the last two words like they burned his tongue. "You need to come to the parade with me. Anyway, church is for Sunday's or holidays." Cameron huffed.

What was it with the Greene men and church services? Donna set her jaw. "I'm honoring my volunteer duties."

Cameron raised his voice. "Do I have to remind you what Jamie did to you and our family?" He pressed his lips into a stern line. When the tips of his ears turned red, Donna knew he'd been stewing for a while over this and wanted to argue.

The old Jamie lived up to everything Cameron said. The present Jamie seemed different. Time and maturity had changed him. She was almost sure of it. Glancing around to get her bearings, she realized they were approaching Eighth Street and were close to Frontier Park. "Let me off here. I'll walk the rest of the way."

"I don't think so. Have you forgotten how Jamie acts? He's a sweet talker and cheater." Cameron remained in the stream of traffic. "Man, he always knew how to play you."

Donna needed to get out of the cab of this pickup. Now. She wrapped her purse strap around her arm and focused on the stoplights. A flash of yellow caught her eye. When the traffic light turned red and the vehicle came to a complete stop, she pressed the unlock button on the door and flicked the handle. Her cowboy boots thumped against the concrete on the street. Her purse slapped against her leg.

"Donna."

She slammed the heavy door shut, cutting off any more of Cameron's opinions. She hurried to the sidewalk before the traffic started back up. After two blocks Donna slowed her pace.

Hefting her purse to her shoulder, she looped the strap over her head and let it hang to her side. The narrow leather pressed against her scar. Donna adjusted the strap and rubbed her chest before lowering her hand.

She should have sought Jamie out after her lumpectomy over a year ago. Regret flooded her heart. She'd have handled it in private without family involvement— the way she had taken care of all the other details during that time. Cameron might enjoy carrying a grudge, she didn't. Especially now that she was actively studying God's word. God wanted people to forgive each other. She'd procrastinated long enough. Before it was too late, she'd tell Jamie she forgave him for his past transgressions. Maybe then he'd leave her alone.

Drawing in a deep breath, she crossed the street and walked through the entrance of Frontier Park. Donna needed the cool morning air to help her clear her head and get her emotions in check before she faced the public *and Jamie* at Cowboy Church.

It'd been a long night. Jamie fought his urge to yawn while once again the young barrel racer poured out her troubles.

"Pastor Martin, I'm not taking your advice lightly."

Here it comes, again.

"But if God wants me to pursue an education, why am I having such a hard time fitting in?"

Jamie swallowed hard. His college experience mirrored the young girl's. Both of them received communications scholarships to universities in urban areas. Hers Boston, his Berkeley. Places where rodeo and rural life seemed hard to understand. There was a big difference, though. She bucked at her peers' image of a barrel racer, while he had buckled under the pressure. Sure he still wore his Stetson and tight Levi's, and joked off their insults. All while becoming a consummate party boy.

"Everyone wants to be accepted, but it's hard. I know you think quitting college is the answer. It's not. You received a full ride for an education in a field you hope to work in. Don't let a few others ruin your future."

"Maybe I should let go of my dream of becoming a news anchorwoman and make my living as a barrel racer."

Jamie placed his hand over the young woman's. "Don't give up on your dream. You obviously worked hard in high school if you earned a full scholarship. Get the education. Give it time. You made it through your freshman year."

The young woman's hand squeezed his. "I did. Maybe I need to rely on God more this fall."

"He won't let you down. I promise." All this girl needed was a firm foundation in Christ, someone to depend on when she felt lost and lonely. "Try joining some organizations, get involved with a local church and let people see what a unique individual you are. Don't allow other people to make you feel like a second-class citizen because of where you were raised."

Jamie earned a smile.

"Thank you, Pastor Martin. You give good advice. I feel so much better than I did last night. Everything in my life seemed so bleak, not fitting in with the Boston crowd, then blowing my run at yesterday's performance."

"I know. We all have trials." Jamie looked up to see Donna walk through the door. Happiness skipped through him at the sight of her yet she represented a trial of his own. He needed her forgiveness and the forgiveness of the entire Greene family.

Donna scanned the room. Her eyes narrowed when they settled in the corner where Jamie ministered to the young barrel racer. She practically stomped across the floor to where Grant stood. Jamie furrowed his brows. Had his behavior at the rodeo yesterday caused this reaction? He'd been so caught up in the moment it seemed natural to share a kiss with the woman he loved. Jamie swallowed hard. Donna didn't know he still loved her though, did she? He knew his need for her forgiveness was twofold—to complete his sobriety step and to win back her love. After twenty years he still pined for the love they once shared.

"Pastor Martin?"

"I'm sorry. What did you say?" Jamie turned his attention back to the young lady.

"I asked if you'd say a prayer for me."

"Of course." Jamie removed his hat and balanced it on one knee. He covered their clasped hands with his free hand and bowed his head.

"Lord, You have a sheep who feels lost in Your world. Call to her heart and lead her down Your path where she'll feel accepted, loved and successful. Let her know the plans You have for her. Plans that include good things. Things she can't even imagine at this stage in her life. Help her turn to You in troubled times and trust You in all areas of her life. Keep her safe and secure. We pray this in your name. Amen."

"Amen." The young woman's eyes met Jamie's. She blinked away a film of moisture covering them. It was a prayer Jamie wished someone had prayed for him during his college years. If he'd only turned to God for courage then instead of an alcohol-induced false bravado.

Jamie pulled his hands away. "You come back anytime during the rodeo, and promise me you'll find a home church in Boston." He placed his felt hat back on his head.

"I will." A wide smile lit the girl's face and brightened her blue eyes.

Smiling on the outside, Jamie sighed inside, hoping he'd made a difference in her mind-set.

She walked to the doorway, turned and waved Jamie's way. He held up his palm to return her gesture. When she exited, he closed his tired eyes and mopped his face with his hands. The older he got the harder it was to pull an all-nighter, but he did what he had to do. In most cases a troubled soul just needed to be heard.

He stretched his arms over his head and down his sides, arching his back to relieve his stiff muscles. He'd heard Grant making phone calls and knew he had rearranged volunteer schedules to accommodate this change in Jamie's.

Jamie would need to leave soon to get some shut-eye before today's rodeo performance. However, spending time volunteering with Donna might be the energizer he needed. Stuffing his hands in his back pockets, Jamie walked over to the makeshift reception desk where Donna sat reading.

"Good morning." Jamie noted the title of the devotional book she held in her hand.

Donna glanced up from her reading. A dull veil hung over her caramel-brown eyes just before they narrowed slightly. "'Morning." Her pretty lips drew into a deep frown.

Jamie's heart dropped to his stomach faster than a roped calf hit the arena dirt. Distrust mixed with anger formed the curtain covering her pretty features. He thought he'd made progress toward seeking her forgiveness, but judging by Donna's forbidding body language and unfriendly tone, he'd really messed up.

Chapter 7

It was such a nice night. Donna wanted to sit outside and enjoy the evening air sans the humidity that came with late July nights in Nebraska. She clenched and unclenched her fists while she peered out her camper window. No sign of life in the neighboring camper. She didn't want to run into Jamie. Another pastor filled the pulpit at the evening worship service. Jamie was probably out on a date with a certain young woman.

What a fool she'd been, ready to forgive Jamie for his past sins. Toying with the idea God might be granting them a second chance at love.

She huffed. Wasn't part of her plan after her diagnosis to stop living a sheltered life? She'd hidden from Jamie for twenty years and now here she was cowering in her camper so she wouldn't have to face him again.

Standing straight, Donna grabbed her Bible off the counter and tugged on the hem of her oversized T-shirt making sure it fell to midthigh over her yoga pants. A wave of foolishness crashed over her heart. Her days of feeling feminine ended over a year ago. The glimmers of attraction Jamie's eyes cast her way tricked her into thinking she could *and should* try to catch a man's eye. Until she'd walked into the tent and saw Jamie, still dressed in yesterday's clothing and holding a young woman's hand. The girl had smiled at him as if he was the only man in the world.

Memories of Jamie's many flirtations had rushed back. Compared to the willowy young woman who wore skin-tight jeans and a formfitting T-shirt, she felt frumpy. So why not dress the part?

Opening the camper door, Donna sized up the neighboring camper. Open windows revealed no muted conversation, no drone from a television or music humming from a radio. Convinced no one was home, Donna stepped outside.

Dusk draped the sun necessitating a light to read. Donna pulled her chair close to a hook where a battery operated camping lantern hung. Switching it on, she opened her Bible to the place she'd left off two mornings ago in second Corinthians.

Her gaze drifted to the Bible verse that spoke to her heart urging her to forgive Jamie. "Therefore if anyone is in Christ, he is a new creation; the old has gone, the new has come!"

Jamie certainly seemed as if he had Christ in his heart. He did seem sincere in his apology for his past mistakes, yet she'd caught him red-handed this morning. So was the old Jamie really gone?

God's word blurred as disappointed tears welled in her eyes. Cameron might enjoy holding a grudge, she didn't. She didn't want Cameron to be right about Jamie still being a liar and cheater. She wanted to prove to Cameron that he was wrong. And she'd planned to until she walked into Cowboy Church and saw Jamie living up to Cameron's expectations.

The roar of a diesel engine startled Donna. She swiped the moisture from her eyes with the back of her hand. Dustin didn't need to see her in this melancholy state.

The vehicle door clicked open, then closed. Donna kept her head down until her cheeks and eyes were dry.

"Hi, Donna. We saw your light and decided you might like some company."

Donna's shoulders sagged. It wasn't Dustin.

It was Jamie.

The pickup engine chugged once before it went silent. Then another door clicked open and thunked closed. Donna looked up. At Grant.

Both men had changed clothes. Grant wore a green plaid short-sleeved Western shirt with faded jeans. Jamie wore a brown T-shirt with a screen-printed Celtic cross on the front paired with dark brown denim jeans.

"Evening, ma'am." Grant tipped his hat and looked around. "Got another chair at your place?" He directed his question at Jamie who started to slide onto the other lawn chair.

"Sure do, right around the corner."

Donna watched Grant retreat to the other side of Jamie's camper. He rounded back with two hard plastic chairs in his hands. Obviously, they intended to stay even though she'd extended no greeting or welcome.

"Never know when someone else might happen by." Grant set the chairs side by side facing Donna and Jamie. He took a seat across from Donna.

"Did you enjoy your volunteer hours today?" Grant brushed a hand down his moustache.

Donna tilted her head. "You know, I did." She refrained from adding a retort about the young girl holding Jamie's hand.

She noted the confused expression on Jamie's face. "Really?"

The corner of Donna's lip quivered, threatening to break into a smile. She'd been brusque with Jamie but she'd enjoyed visiting with the tourists, cowboys and other volunteers. "Yes, very much. I couldn't believe how quickly the three hours flew by."

"That's good." Grant smiled. "So you'll be back."

Is this the reason they stopped? To find out if they'd lost a volunteer? "Yes. I'll be back tomorrow."

Jamie's relieved smile caused Donna's lips to quirk into a grin.

"I thought I'd be sharing a shift with both of you, but you seemed to disappear about thirty minutes after I arrived." Donna wanted to make sure Jamie knew she'd seen him with the young woman. "A breakfast date, perhaps?"

"No…um…" Jamie fell silent for a minute. "Duty called."

Odd. Jamie stumbled over his explanation. The old Jamie's alibis had rolled off his tongue like the fables of a practiced oral storyteller.

"Yep, changed our schedule. It usually happens once a rodeo." Grant gripped the arms of the plastic chair and tipped it back on two legs.

"Speaking of rodeo. Did you go to the performance today?"

Donna nodded. "Not such a good day for any of the contestants. I think the heat affected the animals. It was tough for the ropers, I'm sorry to say. The calves loped from the chutes and made it hard for them."

"That's what Blake said. It's good news for our boys, though. They're still first and second on the leaderboard." Jamie nodded his head.

"Yes, it is. Aunt Donna, are you having a party and forgot to invite me?"

Dustin stood in the shadows between Donna's camper and Grant's pickup, hands on his hips. Donna's heart cantered. She scanned the darkness looking for Cameron's silhouette, which would surely lead to disaster.

"Come join us. We have an empty chair."

"I believe it's Aunt Donna who should be inviting me in, not you." Dustin glared down at Jamie when he passed by. Dustin bent down and pecked a kiss on Donna's cheek. Donna caught the rise of Grant's bushy brows and the pointed look he shot Jamie.

"I didn't see you drive up." Donna watched Dustin fold his lanky frame onto the vacant chair.

"I'm not surprised. The vet's truck blocks most of the view of the street." Dustin glared at Jamie. "I didn't see lights on in the camper and wondered what was going on."

Donna gasped. "Dustin." She put a hand to her chest.

Her nephew answered her with raised palms.

Before she could scold him for being rude, Jamie's even tone cut through the thickening silence. "We were rehashing today's tie-down roping event and how well you faired yesterday."

Dustin nodded. "Second. Not quite first. I can live with it. Blake is giving me a run for my money. If he keeps this up, he'll have some sponsors in no time."

Jamie nodded and smiled.

"What do you think of the Hawthorne fellow?" Grant crossed his arms over his chest.

"He's a loner. He's fast, though, his horse and his hands." Dustin stretched out his legs, crossing them at the ankle.

Jamie leaned forward in his chair. "In all my years announcing rodeo, I've never seen a horse come out of the gate as fast as his does and never break the barrier."

"I guess I never noticed."

"Seems odd to me." Jamie sat back in his chair.

"You think that's where he's gaining time on Blake and me?"

"I do."

Donna rolled her eyes. "It's not his horse. It's his tie-down. His hands fly tying the half hitch."

"I don't know. His horse seems unnaturally fast."

"Well, you have the right to your opinion, Jamie." Donna looked over at him. "I have seen some fast horses in my day."

"However Hawthorne makes his time, he's a threat to Blake and me."

Donna marveled at Dustin's lack of ambivalence toward Jamie the more they discussed rodeo. It didn't get him off the hook. There were two things on her list now to discuss in private with her godson.

"Speaking of fast horses, the Appaloosa the blonde barrel racer rides is fast. Did you see her performance yesterday?"

"Yeah, she's a beauty. Her horse is, too." Dustin chuckled at his joke, rather his attempt at a joke.

This was the only side of her nephew Donna didn't like. He was a womanizer. It was a harsh word to describe her godson, and it pained her to think it. However, it was true. He hadn't always treated love interests this way. In high school, he'd had a steady girlfriend whom he treated with the utmost respect. Or so it appeared to Donna whenever she visited them in Texas.

To Jamie's credit, he didn't join in Dustin's fun. "She is a lovely girl. I had the privilege to talk to her after yesterday's ride. It was too bad she knocked over the last barrel."

The image of Jamie and the young blonde girl holding hands flashed through Donna's mind. She was the barrel racer they were discussing. A sudden and strong pang of jealousy shot through Donna at the pride sounding in Jamie's voice when he talked about the girl.

Bitter words formed on her tongue. She clamped her lips tight to avoid spitting out the hurt and disgust she felt. Despite her age and maturity level, the green-eyed monster growing in her heart was fierce. Stronger than any pangs of jealousy she felt over rivals making eyes or advances at Jamie in their twenties. She had no ties on Jamie. So why did she feel this way? Maybe it was the ridiculousness of the age difference. The young woman could be his niece or daughter.

Then it hit her like a bull ramming the rodeo clown's barrel. Envy gripped her heart and tried to wring the hope from it. No longer young and seemingly flawless, she lifted her right hand to her chest and rested it over the scarred area. Jamie's attention gave her the hope she could still attract a man despite her surgery. Something she never thought she'd feel again and wanted to hold on to. But if Jamie was involved with another woman…

"What are you doing here?"

Cameron's raised voice echoed through the campsite and snapped Donna out of her thoughts. He stood in front of Jamie, sneering down at him.

"Uncle Cameron, we're discussing today's rodeo performance, that's all."

"I suppose you're sizing up stock too, aren't you, Martin. You know we have a bronco and a bull in contention to go to the National Finals. Are you trying to sweet talk my sister again so you can ruin our stock company?"

In the dim light of the camp lantern, Donna saw Jamie's jaw set. "Like your nephew said, we're discussing today's rodeo events."

"You need to leave and stop hanging around my sister. You've caused enough trouble for the Greene family. I'm not letting you have a repeat performance."

Jamie stood. Donna held her breath. Twenty years ago, he'd have thrown a punch by now. *Twenty years ago, he'd have been drunk by now.*

"Cameron, I've asked your sister to forgive me for what I did in the past. I'm trying to show her I've changed. Now, I'm asking you to let me prove I've changed, and perhaps you can forgive me, too."

"Not a chance." Cameron poked the air between the two men.

In a synchronized motion, Donna and Grant stood, ready to intervene if the two men came to blows. Donna remained planted in front of her chair, while Grant moved to Jamie's side. Although he stood in the shadows, Donna knew Cameron could see him from the corner of his left eye.

Cameron leaned forward in an aggressive stance. Jamie stood tall and relaxed. His arms hung at his sides. His body language reflected no anger. A tickle of pride wrapped through her at Jamie's maturity.

"You may be able to sweet-talk women into forgiving you." Cameron glanced narrow-eyed at Donna before turning his attention back to Jamie. "It won't work on me. I don't care about your sobriety. It's too late to help our family." Cameron inched closer to Jamie.

Even in the pale light emitting from the lantern, Donna saw the fight in Cameron's eyes and a steely defiance cover Jamie's beautiful hazel irises, the only sign of defense Jamie displayed.

"You've caused this family enough trouble and duped my sister one too many times."

Dustin stood at the gruffness in Cameron's voice.

"Now get out of here." Cameron leaned his face inches from Jamie's.

Jamie stood very still, his only movement the clench of his jaw. "I believe it's up to Donna whether I leave or not." Jamie's calm and smooth tone surprised Donna. Why, she didn't know. He'd been full of surprises since they'd gotten reacquainted.

"She wants you to leave." Cameron kept his eyes on Jamie.

"I'll go when I hear it from her."

Both men's heads turned simultaneously in Donna's direction. Dustin stepped closer to her, obviously thinking she'd need protection since any answer she gave would be wrong.

She didn't want Cameron bullying Jamie yet after catching Jamie flirting with the young barrel racer, Donna really didn't want to be around him either. Jamie left no doubt in her mind. He had changed. How much, she wasn't certain.

"Jamie." Donna stepped toward the men, pushing her brother's shoulder until he backed up a step or two. "It'd be best if you left."

"All right, if that's what you want, I'll go." Jamie motioned for Grant to move. They both stepped around

Cameron. Jamie cut a path toward the front of his RV. Grant walked to his pickup, slipped behind the wheel and started it up, flooding the scene in bright light.

Cameron's expression shocked Donna. Horrible hatred and anger twisted his features, making him almost unrecognizable. She knew he carried a grudge. After all these years it hadn't diminished?

The diesel engine chugged and the lighted area grew smaller as Grant backed out of the parking spot. Donna expected the light to continue to fade. It didn't. Then she saw why. Jamie had turned around and walked with a determined swagger toward Cameron's back.

Her stomach twisted into a knot tighter than a half hitch. Was Jamie's retreat a trick? Did he plan to catch Cameron off guard? Use an element of surprise to get in the first punch?

She needed to warn her brother. The words of warning forming in her mind clogged in her throat as she watched Jamie bypass Cameron. He stopped in front of her and pushed his Stetson up to reveal his forehead. Donna knew that move. Her heart started to race.

With a quick fluid movement, Jamie pulled her into his arms.

Donna managed to rest her palms against Jamie's chest before he closed the gap between them. She felt the erratic pulse of his heart. Lifting her head, she searched his face before looking into his eyes. She released a shaky breath. Did she see a flicker of love dancing in Jamie's eyes? Before she could be certain, Jamie dropped his gaze to her lips.

Her breathing became rapid when he angled his head.

The image of Jamie and the young barrel racer popped into her mind. *Push away.*

Jamie tightened his embrace as if he'd read her mind,

then he pressed his lips against hers. Time twirled around her, transporting her back twenty years. A thrill danced through her, swirling away the years and heartache, leaving her to feel young and daring and happy. When she slid her arms around Jamie's neck, he deepened the kiss. She drank in his tenderness and warmth. Nothing mattered but this moment. She remembered this feeling. Warm and cozy and comfortable. It felt like home.

As Donna began to meld her body against Jamie, he jerked away breaking all physical contact.

"Leave my sister alone," Cameron growled as he shoved Jamie.

The gravel in the parking area crunched under Jamie's boots as he skidded to regain his balance.

In an instant, Dustin pushed himself between the two men. "Uncle Cameron, enough. This is Aunt Donna's decision to make."

Donna didn't have time to interject and tell her brother to leave or to ask Jamie to stay. Dustin turned on his heel. "I really do think you should go." Although his command was firm, his voice held no anger or malice toward Jamie.

Jamie nodded, looked past Dustin and tipped his hat toward Donna.

Cameron took a step toward Jamie. Dustin held his ground and pushed his uncle back. "You need to cool off."

"Oh, you think so? You don't know how it feels to struggle. To get up before dawn and work hard all day with barely anything to show for it. But your grandpa did. Then when a ray of hope presented itself, a chance to lift his stock company up to the bigger leagues in rodeo, some old drunk—" Cameron yelled the words toward Jamie's camper "—ruined it for him!"

Cameron turned his fury on Donna. "But you know how it feels to shop in secondhand stores or wear home-made clothes because you can't afford new ones. You knew what Old Dependable meant to the family. To Dad."

"I didn't have anything to do with the accident. You can't pin the blame on me. You were the one Dad appointed guardian of the livestock." Donna stated her defense in a matter-of-fact tone. After the kiss Jamie planted on her and the excitement coursing through her, she found it very hard to return Cameron's anger. She fingered her tingling lips and fought a smile, which she knew would just rile up Cameron.

"If you take up with him again, you aren't honoring Dad's memory."

She'd had enough of her older brother. Donna pointed toward his pickup. "Do you want to talk about honoring Dad's memory? I doubt he'd appreciate the way you talked to his one and only grandson. It's not Dustin's fault the Bliss family has money."

Warmth covered her shoulder as Dustin gave it a gentle squeeze. "Thanks, Aunt Donna. I'll walk him to his pickup and follow him out of here."

Donna waved a dismissive hand at her brother. "Go back to the hotel, Cameron. He only kissed me to get back at you, to make you angrier. And it worked."

Cameron glared at her, but turned when Dustin walked up beside him. Donna watched the men walking away from her and smiled. Jamie knew kissing her would incite Cameron's temper. Deep down Donna hoped it wasn't the only reason he'd kissed her.

She opened the camper door and glanced over her shoulder. No lights shone from the narrow windows. She imagined Jamie left them off and was peering out into the night to make sure she was all right. Or maybe he stood in the shadows.

"That was some kiss, Jamie Martin."

A soft giggle hiccupped from her. She couldn't remember the last time she'd experienced this bubbling happiness. She planned to hold on to it. At least for tonight.

Chapter 8

Jamie stood outside of Donna's camper door, shifting his weight from one foot to the other while his mind argued with his heart about whether this was a good idea. It was early. He didn't hear any movement within the compact temporary home. He could leave now and she'd never know he was here. *Knock!*

Twelve hours had passed since he'd seen Donna and the taste of her returned kiss still lingered on his lips. His heart tipped the scales. He wanted, no needed, to see her again. He hoped she felt the same way. He sucked in his breath as a rope of fear noosed his heart. He raised his fisted right hand and lightly tapped against the door.

Within seconds, Donna's footsteps padded in the camper. "Jamie, what are you doing here at this hour?"

Jamie couldn't see Donna's face, but her voice came from the vicinity of the kitchenette's window.

Easing his hat brim up as if it would assist him in seeing her through the window screen, Jamie fixed his eyes in the area where he thought Donna stood. "Blake and I are heading into Cheyenne for the pancake breakfast. We thought you might want to join us."

His pulse drummed so hard in his ears, he doubted he'd be able to hear Donna's reply.

She leaned toward the window. "I'll need five minutes."

Jamie opened his mouth to rebut her refusal. He knew she ate a healthy breakfast of oatmeal most days… He pulled a face. "Did you say yes?"

Lilting laughter tinkled out through the window. "I did if you can give me five minutes."

"Sure. Of course." Jamie smiled at Donna's hazy silhouette through the window screen.

"I'll meet you over at your camper in a few minutes."

"Okay."

Jamie leaned against the fender of the pickup, while Blake waited behind the wheel. True to her word, Donna showed up at five minutes on the dot. Jamie blinked twice. Most people who visited the rodeo dressed in Western clothes. Not Donna, not today. She wore a purple cropped pants outfit and multicolored butterflies graced her earlobes.

He liked the look. Jamie opened the passenger door of the pickup.

"Ah, so we're riding the cowboy way? At least by sitting in the middle, I won't have to get out to open and close the gate." Donna winked at Jamie and scooted into the cab of the vehicle. Her flowery fragrance wafted with her movements. Light and summery, it accentuated her outfit and sparked the memory of their kiss last night. Her fragrance filled his senses and height-ened the pleasure of their kiss. He closed his eyes and inhaled deeply, memorizing the scent. He knew he'd always associate a gardenia's fragrance with Donna and last night's kiss.

Once Donna was situated and buckled up, Jamie crawled into the passenger seat. Most of the time Jamie enjoyed the roominess of the crew cab, today he wished it was smaller, more intimate. It wouldn't hurt his feelings to brush shoulders with Donna.

Blake put the truck into gear and backed out onto the street. "Sorry you have to sit in the middle. I stashed my gear and chaps in the back. Since it's a dry year here at the Daddy of 'em All, I'm afraid the seat is dusty."

"It's okay. I've ridden this way many times in my life. Plus, a hitchhiker can't be too choosy." Donna smiled at Blake, who put the truck in Drive and started off.

"Well, it doesn't make sense for your family..." Jamie stopped and swallowed hard. He didn't want to wreck Donna's good mood, although she did seem a bit too cheerful this morning. He'd worried last night's events might put more tension between them. He cleared his throat. "To drive clear out here to pick you up."

Donna cast him a sideways look and shrugged, her shoulder brushing against his. Tingles began at the point of impact, turning into full-fledged ripples down his arm.

"You're right. I don't think Cameron or Dustin realized how far away from their hotels I'd be. I figured I'd miss the pancake breakfasts after Cameron appointed Dustin my driver." Donna started laughing. "There is absolutely no way Dustin gets up until nine o'clock in the morning, unless it's to travel to a rodeo."

"Oh, to be young again." Jamie heard the wistfulness in his voice. At Dustin's age, he hadn't been an early riser either due to partying all night or sleeping off a drunk. There was so much he'd do differently now, if he could go back. Starting with Donna.

"Hey, now. I've always gotten up early." Blake shot Jamie a look of mock aggravation before turning his attention back to traffic.

"I'm not faulting Dustin. I do remember the days of being carefree with no responsibilities and sleeping in every morning. Now those days are few and far between. I do want to thank you both for thinking of me this morning."

Although Donna included both of them in her appreciation, she looked directly at Jamie. For the first time since last night's events, their eyes met. Something unmistakable shone from Donna's eyes. Jamie wanted it to be love for him, but it was something else. Contentment or peace, maybe?

He needed to talk to her. He'd heard what she told Cameron. But Jamie didn't kiss her to make Cameron angrier. He'd wanted to kiss her, had wanted to kiss her since he realized who neighbored their camper. Raising Cameron's ire was just an added bonus.

Jamie wanted Donna to understand he wasn't using her to get back at her brother or to gain the Greene family's forgiveness. It was her forgiveness and love he needed. He cared for her, deeply. He always had and he always would.

"Here we are." Blake pulled into a parking spot at the Depot Plaza. The area buzzed with cowboys and tourists all after the free pancake breakfast.

"How early do you have to get here to beat the crowd?" Jamie opened his door, slid from the seat and held a hand out to assist Donna from the vehicle.

She slipped her palm into his and stepped on the

running board before stepping to the ground. "I can get out of a pickup unassisted, you know." She moved to the side so Jamie could close the door. "However, your gesture was nice and very gentlemanly of you, Jamie Martin." Her wide smile deepened the lines around her eyes and the love in Jamie's heart.

Pride puffed out Jamie's chest until he thought a snap on his Western shirt might pop open. He'd worried, then prayed, last night for Donna not to be angry at him for kissing her or sorry she returned his kiss. He guessed the Lord had answered his prayer because Donna seemed more than amicable today. But Jamie never had a chance to talk to Donna about it as they stood in line waiting. People constantly stopped to chat to Donna, Blake or him

Jamie couldn't help but notice the attention the Hardin girl paid to Blake, her assertiveness a contrast to Blake's bashful nature. And he didn't miss his nephew's subtle signs of interest in Brittney.

Jamie was lost in thought as they found seats and began to eat.

"Hey, are you guys about ready to go?" Blake asked.

Jamie looked across the table at Blake and his empty plate. Hadn't they just sat down to eat? He glanced to his left. Donna had eaten only half of her breakfast.

"Or do you need a ride back to your camper, Donna? I'd be happy to wait and take you."

Blake must have noticed Jamie assessing the situation.

"I'm here for the day or at least until the rodeo performance is over." Donna cut a bite from her pancake. "You two go on. I'm sure I can catch a shuttle or cab to Frontier Park or get my walk in for the day."

Raising his brows, Blake looked at Jamie. Frontier Park was quite a ways from the historic railroad depot.

"I'll stay with Donna." Jamie hitched his thumb toward the back of a long line of people. "Grant will give us a ride back to the rodeo grounds."

"Okay, see you both later." Blake tipped his hat to Donna and left.

Jamie dug back into his short stack. This would be his chance to explain his actions last night.

When they were finished eating, Jamie collected the plates and utensils and threw them in the trash.

"I'd really like to walk, but Frontier Park is pretty far." Donna looked down at Jamie's cowboy boots, then back up. "It's okay if you don't want to join me."

"I'll be okay unless you're planning to speed walk."

Donna chuckled. "I am a walker. I usually put in three to five miles a day, either outside or on my treadmill."

Jamie raised his brows. "I'll text Grant our route so he can pick us up after he's through eating. That should give us thirty to forty minutes."

"Okay. If I get clipping along too fast for you, tell me and I'll slow down." Donna took a step. Jamie fell in beside her.

"What I might need is a little guidance with directions. So much has changed since I was here last. Twenty years is a long time." Donna craned her neck looking both ways.

It certainly is. Determined to keep the mood light, Jamie didn't voice his thought. "Don't worry I'll point you in the right direction, unless I keel over from too much exercise." Jamie smiled.

"Well, a little more exercise would help with your high blood pressure and cholesterol."

"That's true." Was Donna concerned about him? Hope flipped Jamie's heart. The thought boosted his confidence to broach the subject he knew they were both hinting at yet dancing around.

"Say, about last night."

Donna's abrupt stop caught Jamie off guard. He walked two steps, then had to take two steps back to face her.

"Don't tell me you regret it." Donna's low tone held an edge of fierceness. "Or there is someone else in your life."

Jamie lifted his hands in the air palms out. "Not. At. All. On both accounts."

The memory of her soft lips yielding under his forced a wide smile to his lips.

"Oh." Donna grinned. Her shoulder's relaxed. She took a step.

"I heard what you told Cameron. That I only kissed you to make him angry."

"So you were hanging around in the shadows? I knew I didn't hear your door latch."

"Yeah, I leaned against the front of my camper, out of everyone's line of sight. I wanted to make sure you were okay."

A tender look crossed Donna's face. She lifted a hand to her chest as if to still her beating heart, then a sheen of sadness settled on her features.

Jamie's brows knitted at her strange reaction. "I want you to know what you said wasn't true. I wanted to kiss you and let you know someone was on your side. Cameron doesn't treat you with respect. He never did." Jamie cringed at his own words. Twenty years ago, he thought he was treating Donna with respect, too. In hindsight he hadn't.

"So, you weren't staking a claim?" A gentle breeze blew silver strands of Donna's hair across her eyes. She reached up a hand and fingered them back into place.

"Hmm…" He didn't mean to hum his answer. Her simple movement created a reaction in him. He itched to run his fingers through her hair. Feel its texture now that she wore it natural and not chemically treated. Her style framed her face and her hair looked soft and silky. He longed to confirm his suspicion.

What would her reaction be, if he stopped right here on the sidewalk, ran his fingers through her hair, cupped her face and kissed her? His heart raced at the thought. *Whoa.* How respectful would that be? Hadn't he just criticized her brother's disrespectful treatment of her?

Jamie stuffed his hands in his pockets, confining them, and hopefully his thoughts, from action.

They reached a street corner and stopped with a crowd waiting for the light to change.

Once they crossed the street and the crowd broke up, Donna turned to him. "You didn't answer my question."

Jamie drew a ragged breath. He wanted nothing more than to stake a claim on Donna's heart. He knew now that was not the way love worked. He couldn't win her love by conquering her. He wanted her to love him on her own terms. "I was letting you know how much I care for you, not staking a claim. The truth is I have always cared for you."

For a few seconds, Donna continued to stare straight ahead. Didn't she realize he'd laid himself bare?

Happiness expanded in Jamie's heart when she slipped her hand in his.

* * *

"Grant and I have a couple of things we need to do. Promise me you'll meet me by the portal ten entrance of the grandstand at eleven-thirty."

"I promise." Donna crossed her heart with the index finger of her left hand.

Jamie squeezed her hand before he released it and strode off in the direction of the animal pens.

Donna needed to rein in her emotions. She didn't want to send mixed signals to Jamie, build up hope in his heart for a love that probably could never be. Yet she did enjoy his kiss. It woke her heart up. Reminded her of what she'd been missing. What she didn't know was whether she missed him or just missed having an emotional connection with someone of the opposite sex. It'd been such a long time since she last rode around the arena of love. After being bucked off in her twenties, she'd never freely given her entire heart to anyone. Was that why Jamie's kiss felt so different and wonderful?

Turning toward the vendor booths, Donna planned to browse away the morning. The first vendor she happened on sold bright-colored saddle blankets displayed attractively on shelving designed to look like rustic fence posts. She seldom rode a horse anymore and smiled at the irony of a stockman's daughter and sister preferring to help out on the ranch only if she could use an ATV.

In the next area, Donna spent quite a bit of time browsing through the merchandise. The vendor sold horseshoes, twisted and welded into Western art and home furnishings. Donna decorated her home office with a Western flair, while the remainder of her home was an eclectic mix of contemporary furnishings.

She'd guessed Jamie decorated his ranch with masculine Western decor.

Giving her head a little shake, Donna gave herself a mental scolding. One kiss shouldn't lead to the thoughts she'd been having all night wondering about Jamie's life and whether she might fit into it. Happiness tickled through her. She moved on to the next vendor booth.

"Hi." The pretty blonde barrel racer who'd held Jamie's hand the other day stood on the opposite side of a clothing rack.

Donna managed a weak smile while her happy heart deflated in her chest.

"Didn't I see you at the FCC tent?"

"Yes."

"Are you a pastor, too?"

"No. I'm a volunteer."

"Isn't this pretty?" The girl held up a purple plaid Western-cut shirt with white piping. She laid it over her chest. "Purple is my favorite color."

"It's very nice." Donna had always favored the deep darts in Western blouses that gave them their formfitting design. Until a year ago. Now she tugged on the hem of her blouse and tried to fight feeling frumpy beside the barrel racer, who wore tight blue jeans and a sheer sleeveless shirt over a snug tank top.

"Do you know Pastor Martin?" The young woman glanced her way before scrutinizing the shirt's quality and checking the price tag.

"Yes, I do."

Dreamy eyed, the barrel racer looked at Donna. "He's something, isn't he?"

Donna leaned forward. Had the girl sighed? How should she answer her? The young woman looked barely nineteen or twenty—much too young for Jamie. Was there a delicate way to tell this girl that? Or was it even Donna's place to say something?

Donna puckered her lips. Honestly, if she gave man advice to this girl regarding Jamie, it was selfish and not out of concern. Donna couldn't compete with a twenty-year-old and she knew it. In reality, she couldn't compete with women her own age anymore. She lifted a hand and patted her chest.

"Wow, you didn't answer me. Does that mean you don't like him? He gave me some advice, but maybe I shouldn't take it."

The young woman had mistaken her silence.

"I want to be a television journalist someday." Replacing the hanger on the rack, she pulled out a fringed and sequined blouse. "This is too much bling." She wiggled the hanger and the fringe bounced. "And thanks to Pastor Martin, I'm going to do it."

"What?" Donna pulled her brows together, then tried to relax her features so she didn't appear rude or suspicious. Was Jamie paying for her schooling? "I'm sorry, but what do you mean?" Her poker face held together; her voice betrayed her.

"I got a four year scholarship to school in Boston. I finished my freshman year two months ago and decided to quit college." She reracked the blouse. "I'm too country for the Ivy League school. I don't fit in." She released a heavy sigh. "I can't afford to go to another school, so I was going to give up my scholarship, quit school and earn my living barrel racing. Pastor Martin and I talked all night. He convinced me not to quit school, suggested options for me to try to fit in, then we prayed about it."

This explained Jamie's blurry eyes the other morning. He hadn't been trying to keep up with a young thing. He'd been trying to keep the barrel racer on track. By the sound of it he was successful. Today's youth surprised Donna with their openness and willingness to tell their life stories. She saw it all the time on campus. "What did he suggest?"

"He told me to find and get involved with a church. He said if I gave up my dream and my scholarship, I'd regret it the rest of my life. Then he told me a funny thing about having a dream."

"People will support you, but no one will believe in the dream the way you do," Donna said.

"Right! Isn't it awesome advice?"

Donna's knees went weak. She needed to sit down. She nodded and smiled at the young woman who had no idea how her words affected Donna. Jamie had told Donna the same thing years ago. It was one reason she'd fallen in love with him. He believed in following dreams. It was advice she now wished she'd taken. Swallowing the lump of emotion in her throat, she forced a lightness to her voice. "It is awesome advice. Good luck with your future."

Waiting until the young woman was engrossed in another garment, Donna wandered away from the clothing vendor. She searched the area for a bench. After spotting one a few feet away, she walked to it and sat down. She closed her eyes and bowed her head.

Lord, please forgive me for misjudging Jamie and this young woman's relationship and allowing my jealousy and hurt to get in the way of forgiving Jamie. I believe in Your word. I see Jamie holds You in his heart and I can tell he is a new man. Help me to forgive Jamie in the way You forgave me of my sins. Amen.

The only dreamer in the Greene family, Donna had wanted to travel and work in the tourism field. But hers was a family who all played it safe, each generation making their living in the same business as the last. She didn't follow through with her dreams. She had a good job and nice home. It was a life to be proud of, yet it held regret. She'd listened to the wrong people. It was funny how one accident she wasn't even involved in had changed the course of her life.

Chapter 9

"Good morning." Jamie cuffed Grant's shoulder.

"Morning." Grant made an exaggerated point of searching Jamie's face. "No black eyes, I see. You must have managed to stay out of trouble last night. Unlike Monday night."

"Ha." Jamie filled his response with droll sarcasm and joined Grant looking through the fence rails of the pens at some calves.

"What are you doing down here in the stock pens?"

"I want to talk to Cameron. Apologize for what happened on Monday evening." Jamie planned to make amends with Cameron. No more putting it off.

"Remember you have no control over his forgiveness over both incidents. Did you apologize to Donna?"

Jamie's smile widened. "I tried to. She actually acted angry I'd consider apologizing for my roguish behavior."

Grant wiggled his bushy eyebrows. "That is good

news. Has she forgiven you for your past indiscretions? Helped you complete your sobriety step?"

"No." Jamie rubbed his chin. "I think she will. We held hands today."

"No wonder your smile is ear to ear and you're ready to do something dumb. Love's bravado is coursing through your veins so you want to confront Cameron. You think you're ten feet tall and bulletproof."

Jamie shrugged. "Maybe. Or maybe it's time to clear the air."

"Suit yourself." Grant waved his hand toward the pen holding the bucking horses. "There he is."

Jamie felt Grant's eyes following him as he zig-zagged around the metal fencing panels and headed toward Cameron. Thankfully, no other stockmen were around. They could have a private conversation.

The hard look Cameron shot Jamie stopped him in his tracks and gave him momentary pause. Jamie closed his eyes. *Give me strength, Lord, to handle this difficult situation with diplomacy. Amen.*

Jamie drew a deep breath, squared his shoulders, and walked over to Cameron. "Look, we need to talk."

Cameron continued to inspect the flank of a quarter horse.

"We've needed to talk for a long time," Jamie added.

Cameron lifted his head, his brown eyes dull with loathing and distrust. Jamie swallowed hard. It was difficult to believe they were once colleagues and friends. *And almost brothers-in-law.*

"At least hear me out." Jamie took the slight twitch of Cameron's left eyebrow as an invitation to continue. "I am sorry about the truck accident twenty years ago. I know losing that bull devastated your family and set back your business. It was your company's first chance to have an animal involved at the National Finals."

Jamie paused in case Cameron wanted to accept his apology. After a moment of silence, Jamie continued. "I hope you can find it in your heart to forgive me. I thank God every day no one else was killed due to my negligence."

Cameron's snort echoed through the animal pens. "What you are is lucky my father didn't press charges."

"I am grateful. I didn't act like it then when he fired me, but I was grateful." Jamie rubbed his chin with his thumb and index finger. Was it a good sign Cameron was talking? "Honestly, I don't remember much about that night. I never have. Donna and I had an argument, which is why she didn't go out with us after the rodeo. You had met the town's rodeo queen there."

Cameron's head popped up. He shouted, "No!" He looked around the area. "You met the rodeo queen, not me." He lowered his voice. "She was sitting between us in the cab of the stock truck, remember?"

Jamie closed his eyes and shook his head. "I don't. I don't remember getting behind the wheel of the truck."

The hoarse whisper of his voice transported him back to the past. Time hazed the memory. Alcohol blurred the truth. He'd sat on a bar stool and stumbled when he slid off, grabbing on to the neighboring stool to regain his balance. With concerted effort, he trailed behind the beautiful girl and Cameron when they left the bar. The cold bite in the air shocked him sober. Or at least it was what he must have thought, since he got behind the wheel of the stock truck.

Jamie slowly lifted his lids. Cameron's eyes had narrowed to slits. "That's because you were drunk and insisted on getting behind the wheel. I tried to stop you.

I tried to talk you into leaving the rodeo queen behind, but you threw a punch that knocked me out. I've wished a million times you'd have left me lying on the ground instead of loading me into the vehicle and taking off only to jump the curb and roll the truck. You killed our championship bull, wrecked our new stock truck and cheated on my sister. All of us are lucky to be alive. I will never forgive you. You were a drunk and always will be."

Cameron's voice held such vehemence that Jamie staggered back against a fence. Cameron stalked off and left Jamie leaning against the warm metal with a powerful thirst for a cold, stiff drink.

One little sip of alcohol would burn the edge off his frustration at his blurred memory and his anger at Cameron's recollection of the accident. Nothing Cameron said helped him remember or understand his actions that long ago night. He was failing this step in his sobriety, so why bother anymore? The only member of the Greene family he might earn forgiveness from was Donna. And she hadn't said it yet.

He licked his lips and scanned his mind's map of the area around Frontier Park trying to locate the nearest tavern so he could release this pent-up anxiety.

"So, what are you thinking about?"

Jamie's body jerked at the sound of Grant's voice. Shame warmed his blood. He'd let his memories bring him down and allowed Cameron to throw his pride on the ground and half hitch it until Jamie thought the only way to set himself free was to take a drink.

The ragged breath he released scared a whinny from a horse and sent it trotting around the pen. "I don't have to answer your question." Jamie looked into his friend's concern filled eyes. "You know."

Grant nodded his head and puckered his lips, his moustache covering his mouth like drapes on a window.

Companionable silence surrounded them for a few minutes. "You've done your part. You've asked for forgiveness. It's all you can do. You can't make Cameron forgive you." Grant's blue eyes searched Jamie's face.

"I know."

"Is not having his forgiveness worth falling off the wagon?"

"No."

"Right answer." Grant motioned for Jamie to follow him. "We're going to be late for the noon rodeo."

Jamie fell into step with Grant. "What I'd really like from Cameron is a detailed account of the night of the accident. Maybe it'd help me remember and I could understand."

"And forgive yourself?" Grant stopped.

"I thought I had. Seeing Donna and her family, a family I wanted to be a part of, well, it brings back old regrets."

"Look, you've been sober ten years. Don't let ten days ruin it. I'm here to talk you through anything, buddy. Maybe it isn't me you need to be talking to." Grant pointed a chubby index finger toward the sky. "Pastor Martin, have you spent much time in prayer since Donna parked her camper beside yours?"

"You know the answer to that question, too." Jamie shook his head. "Thanks for the reminder. It might be best if you sat with Donna and me at the rodeo today." His urge to take a drink hadn't dissipated even though Grant was trying to talk him through it.

When Jamie spotted Donna waiting by the entrance for him, he sucked in a hard breath. He kept his eyes riveted on her.

He'd only left her two hours ago. She was dressed in the same clothing, her hair framed her face in the same way, yet she looked different. Radiant.

When she spotted him coming, she waved to get his attention. Had she thought he hadn't seen her or felt her presence drawing him to her like a bee to an apple blossom?

"Did you have lunch?" Donna wrinkled her brow. "Is something wrong? With me?"

She started fidgeting with her hemline, then the collar of her shirt. Jamie grabbed her hand. "Absolutely nothing is wrong with you."

"Then why are you staring at me?" She looked from Jamie to Grant and back to Jamie.

"Because you're beautiful." Jamie grazed the back of her hand with his lips.

A fiery blush reddened her cheeks. "Thank you." She laced her fingers through his.

Time ticked slowly while Jamie drank in her beauty. He wanted to always remember her this way. Although she had yet to say "I forgive you," Jamie was certain she was on the verge of forgiving him. He was proving to her he was a changed man. Deep in his heart, he hoped she'd also admit she loved him, but if she didn't, this was the image of her he'd cherish until his dying day.

"Jamie, are you okay?"

Again Donna's eyes went from him to Grant. A niggle of worry furrowed her brow.

"I'm okay. Grant managed to get a seat beside us for today's rodeo performance. You don't mind, do you?"

"Of course not." A grin pushed any evidence of concern from Donna's features. "Now will you answer my question? Have you eaten lunch yet?"

* * *

The next day a steady rain pinged against the camper. The rain began falling in the wee hours of the morning and continued through the early afternoon. Donna didn't relish the idea of becoming a soggy mess sitting on the bleachers at the rodeo so she spent the day shopping for a new outfit to wear when she played the piano that night at Cowboy Church.

Turning one way and then the other, Donna scrutinized the new outfit she'd bought on her afternoon shopping trip to Frontier Mall. She'd commandeered the pickup when she dropped Dustin off at the airport. He planned to fly to South Dakota and compete in the Deadwood Days of '76 Rodeo then come back to Cheyenne for his second go around.

Donna giggled at her own silliness and took a step back from the mirror. At a popular women's chain store in the mall she'd purchased a twill capri pants and vest set she'd had her eye on since spring. The blouse was formfitting, something she still wasn't comfortable with. But no one would be able to tell she had extra padding in one bra cup.

She twisted again before slipping the vest over the blouse and zipping it halfway up. She smiled. The outfit looked perfect. The vest gave her enough coverage and bumped up her confidence that no one could tell she'd had a lumpectomy.

Crazy as it seemed, she hoped Jamie's eyes sparked with appreciation when he saw her in this outfit the same way they had yesterday afternoon. Donna pushed silver hoops into her pierced ears and walked into the bathroom to do her hair and makeup, taking extra care with her routine and sending up a silent prayer the drizzle didn't turn into a cloudburst.

Although the clouds threatened rain, the weather held out when she left her camper and drove to Frontier Park. After she found a parking spot on a residential street, Donna headed toward the FCC tent.

"There's our prettiest volunteer now." Jamie looked up from behind the pulpit when Donna walked through the tent's entry.

Donna blushed and hoped Jamie would notice the new outfit. Her cheeks burned when she realized Jamie wouldn't know if it was a new outfit.

He walked over to her. "Green has always been your color. Must be because of your last name." His whisper tickled her neck. He gave her a brief hug before he pulled her to arm's length. Her heart melted under the warmth shining from Jamie's hazel eyes.

It'd been so long since she felt this way. Giddy. Happy. Womanly. "Thank you." Her voice came out husky with emotion.

"Did you come to practice? I've chosen older hymns I think most people know."

"It probably wouldn't hurt to practice a little. I'm not quite used to the portable keyboard." Donna broke their eye contact and glanced over at the instrument.

"Don't worry, you'll do fine." Jamie reached up and brushed his fingers across her cheeks. "Besides, church is the best place to make mistakes because we're all about forgiveness."

Moisture sprang to Donna's eyes at Jamie's flippant comment. In her heart she'd forgiven Jamie days ago. His actions proved he'd changed. Not once had she seen him take a drink of liquor or smelled it on him. His anger was apparent in his confrontation with Cameron, yet he'd controlled it unlike the old Jamie who would have swung at Cameron's first insult. Even when she'd suspected him of wooing the young barrel racer, she'd been wrong. He'd been trying to help the girl keep her life on track.

"Say, would you go to dinner with me after the service?" Jamie raised his hands, palms up. Apprehension settled into the lines of his face. "I know it's last minute. I thought we could get a late supper and take a horse drawn carriage ride before I take you home."

A year ago if a man, any man, had asked Donna out on the spur of the moment, she'd have refused. But one thing her cancer scare had taught her was to seize the moment and be spontaneous. "I would love to go out with you."

The lines of apprehension turned into a broad smile. "It's a date."

For a few moments, Donna and Jamie stood with eyes riveted to each other. She hoped her gaze conveyed the same attraction she was drinking in from his. A date with Jamie. Her chance to offer her forgiveness and tell him how proud she was of him for how his life had turned out and for staying sober.

Only a dozen people showed up for Jamie's evening service. He didn't let the small number mar his enthusiasm for preaching. In a rich baritone, Jamie delivered a rousing sermon about service to Christ that made Donna glad she hadn't ducked out on her volunteer duties at Cowboy Church and renewed her resolve to be more involved in her home church and its missions.

Donna kept busy unplugging the portable keyboard and placing the cover over it while Jamie shook hands and visited with folks on their way out of the tent.

"You'll make sure Blake gets back to the RV park?" Jamie held his hand out to Grant.

"That's not necessary. I have the pickup." Donna smiled at Jamie.

"Great." Grant shook Jamie's hand. "You kids have a good time tonight." Grant winked at Donna, drawing instant heat to her cheeks.

It felt like a first date even though she and Jamie had gone out together many times before. Gone was the cocky youth strutting for attention. Instead, before her stood a man with varied interests who listened to others and seldom spoke of himself.

Had she changed enough that this felt like a first date to Jamie too? Doubt crept through her. Probably not. She had listened to her father and played it safe, keeping close to home and the familiar scenery of eastern Nebraska.

Jamie slipped his hand into hers and led her out of the tent. "I thought we could try the steak place on Little Bear Road."

Donna scanned the horizon. Night's gloaming fell over the park. The carnival's bright neon bulbs lit up the sky. Did Jamie remember their first date? It was after a rodeo in a small Northern California town. She breathed deeply. The sweet and savory aromas and lilting calliope music called up her old memories. "That would be nice…"

"Do I hear a *but*?"

She shrugged and jerked her head toward the carnival. "It's probably sentimental. I was remembering…"

"Our first date." Their joined voices seemed amplified in the cool evening air.

Jamie broke eye contact and took an interest in the twisting toe of his silver-tipped cowboy boot. He was dressed in black jeans and the Western shirt with the embroidered crosses. A black felt Stetson replaced the usual brown one. Donna thought he'd never looked more handsome.

"It's okay." Donna squeezed Jamie's biceps. "We can go to the steak house and take a carriage ride."

Looking up at Donna, one corner of Jamie's mouth pulled into a half grin. "I'm okay with going to the carnival and eating corn dogs for supper. It was my original idea. Then I thought after all this time and well, our past history, you wouldn't want me to re-create our first date."

Her eyes roved his features. She'd missed him more than she'd realized. "I would love to re-create it." Donna smiled and nodded her head.

A full smile lit up Jamie's face. "I believe we need to start with a corn dog and a Coke."

Hand in hand they walked back to the entrance gate, showed their rodeo tickets and entered the carnival area. After walking past the carnival games and around the kids' rides, Donna planted herself on a picnic table beside the corn-dog stand and waited for Jamie to deliver her supper.

Jamie set the food in front of her and slid onto the bench opposite her. He removed his hat and placed it on the table. "Shall I say grace?"

"Please do." Donna tipped her head.

"Lord, thank You for the blessings of renewed relationships, pleasant memories and the food we are about to receive. I promise I will eat healthier tomorrow and take care of my body which is Your temple. Amen."

"Amen. I'm sorry. I never considered carnival food shouldn't be in your diet."

"A big juicy steak isn't either." Jamie bit into his corn dog with the gusto of a starving man.

Donna nibbled on the cornmeal breading wrapped around her hot dog. Nerves jittered her stomach making eating her dinner tricky.

A young cowboy walked by. His swagger reflected the chip on his shoulder. Jamie's eyes followed him through the midway.

"Isn't he the tie-down roper that could beat out our nephews for the final win?" Blake and Dustin remained in the top five for winning overall in tie-down roping.

"He's Grady Hawthorne." Jamie shook his head. "He looks like trouble, and I'm an expert on how trouble looks."

"Pastor Martin, you aren't holding a grudge against a cowboy who might be better than your nephew, are you?" Donna raised a brow.

"His horse seems really fast."

"So you keep saying. Some horses are naturally fast. He probably works with him. It doesn't appear he has a girlfriend and he doesn't pay much attention to buckle bunnies. He's always alone. Maybe he practices a lot." Donna watched the young man saunter down the midway. She thought his aloofness might be a mask to hide his loneliness. "Besides, I still think he gains his time in his half hitch." Donna took a large bite of her corn dog since Jamie had started on his second one.

"His horse never stops dancing and comes out fast."

Donna took a sip of soda. "He hasn't broken the barrier."

"I know, but—" Jamie stopped and held up his hands. "This is not a date conversation. Let's get to eating. It seems to me our dinner is followed with a Ferris wheel ride and some cotton candy."

"Right you are."

They finished eating in silence, threw their trash away and walked toward the carnival's ticket booth.

"Whew! How do parents afford to let their kids ride

these days?" He handed Donna a row of tickets and stuffed his wallet into his back pocket.

"Are you saying sharing a few rides with me isn't worth the price?" Donna laughed.

"No, I'm saying…I'm old. I remember when rides took one fifty-cent ticket." Jamie grabbed Donna's hand and pulled her toward the Ferris wheel.

The carny worker motioned for them to get in. He clicked the bar closed and his coworker shifted the lever sending them on a short, jerky ride.

"Guess we get to do this, oh, twenty more times judging by the line." Jamie rested his forearms over the safety bar.

"Tell me about your ranch. Do you run cattle or horses?"

"Sort of." Jamie leaned back in the seat. They took another short spurt backward. "My ranch houses injured and retired rodeo stock champions."

"Oh!" The moment Donna's surprised sigh left her lips she wished she could pull it back in. She put her fingers over her mouth like she'd let a secret slip. She didn't want to hurt Jamie's feelings or ruin their evening.

The seat rocked again. They were halfway to the top of the wheel. Donna looked closely at the man sitting to her left. He had changed. He'd turned a bad accident and life-changing event into something good. Donna lowered her fingers. "I'm sorry. Please don't be offended or hurt by my response. What a wonderful type of ranch to run!"

When the ride started up again, Jamie mocked a stretch, then put his arm across the back of the seat. "Your surprise didn't offend me. How could you know? Well, unless Cameron told you."

"Cameron knows you house injured and retired

rodeo stock?" Donna glanced down. They were high enough now she could see the layout of Frontier Park. She squeezed the safety bar tight and looked back at Jamie.

Nodding, Jamie set his jaw and looked out over the horizon. "All the stock contractors know. When I first put out word I was running that type of ranch, Cameron started a smear campaign against me."

Anger surged through Donna. She bit her tongue until the ride drew them past the workers and started its skyward ascent. "Why would he do that? Obviously you are trying to make amends for your past mistake." Which was admirable. What was wrong with Cameron?

"You're right I am. There are no words to express how badly I feel about the accident and the aftermath it caused. I can't give enough injured animals a home to make up for the loss I caused you and your family."

Donna cupped Jamie's cheek and turned his face to hers. "I am so proud of you, Jamie. I really am." She intended to tell Jamie she was ready to forgive him. Then his soft lips captured hers, stirring her emotions and replacing all of her thoughts with feelings.

Her eyes fluttered shut. Bursts of love's beautiful colors replaced the harsh neon carnival lights attached to the Ferris wheel when Jamie deepened his kiss. As the ride started to glide downward, Donna's heart and soul fell into love's sweet abyss.

Chapter 10

It took three times for Donna to read the Bible verse of her daily devotion before she really comprehended what she read. She'd had a restless night. She peered out the narrow window in the camper door to see if there was any sign of life at her neighbor's camper.

Happiness danced through her and pushed a wide smile to her lips. She didn't know for certain what the future held for her and Jamie. There was so much they needed to discuss. She hadn't had a chance to tell Jamie she forgave him, and before their relationship progressed any further, she needed to tell him about her lumpectomy. Then there was always the issue of Cameron and perhaps the rest of her family, although her sister, Deanne, was young at the time and only worried about herself. She probably didn't remember the repercussions of the accident—only the unflattering stories her father and Cameron recounted.

A knock on the metal camper door startled Donna back to the present. She hadn't seen anyone approach, although she'd been staring in the vicinity of the door, her mind's eye holding visions of a happy ending for her and Jamie.

She glanced at the time. How had an hour passed? She shook her head and opened the door. "Good Morning, Dustin."

"'Mornin'." Dustin's raspy voice and droopy eyes told "the morning came too early" tale. He'd obviously been out most of the night.

Dustin stepped through the door and sagged into an overstuffed swivel rocker. He'd showered. She could smell his spicy aftershave. He wasn't dressed for today's event, though. He wore sneakers, cargo shorts and a Cheyenne souvenir T-shirt with a baseball cap.

"Early flight or late night?"

"Both."

Donna laid her Bible on the counter and took a deep breath. She'd never messed in other people's relationships because of her own track record. However, she'd witnessed Jamie's good-time Charlie days and really didn't want her godson walking the same path.

"So, tell me, did the wolf lead another innocent sheep astray?"

Dustin's deadpan look warned her not to continue. "Guess I should have had my buddy drop me off at Frontier Park."

Raising her eyebrows at Dustin's tone, Donna crossed her arms over her chest. "Remember I'm your elder, aunt and godmother."

The corner of Dustin's mouth quirked up. "How can I forget? I suppose it is your turn to rag on me about my lifestyle."

Donna slipped into the matching chair. "I'm concerned, Dustin. I know I'm the last person who should give relationship advice. This is so out of character for you. You had a steady girlfriend in high school…"

"Yeah, yeah, yeah." Dustin held up a halting hand. "Look, Aunt Donna, I don't want to talk about it. I know I have a ladies' man reputation. It's not always what it seems. Most things aren't. Take Jamie for instance." Dustin hitched a thumb toward Blake and Jamie's camper.

The reference to Jamie surprised Donna. "I'm not exactly certain what you mean."

Dustin shrugged. "Here's what you do need to know. I'm not drinking or doing drugs of any type. Do I stay out late? Yes. Do I hang around the ladies? Yes. Do I respect women? Yes and I don't take advantage of them or use them." A wistful look crossed Dustin's face. "I know most of the women are interested in Dad's family money and not me."

Reaching out, Donna squeezed Dustin's hand. "I understand your struggle. You're trying to find true love."

"The same way you are." Again, Dustin hitched a thumb in the neighboring camper's direction. "We are more alike than you know."

The grandstand resembled a flower bed full of pink blossoms and the color extended to the chutes, too. Jamie was proud of how the cowboys embraced Thursday's Tough Enough to Wear Pink day to promote breast cancer awareness.

Donna went all out wearing pink from head to toe. She wore a pink gingham blouse with a pink denim vest that matched her pink jeans. A pink checked headband held her hair back and exposed her attractive earlobes ornamented with earrings in the pink ribbon design associated with breast cancer. Even her cowboy boots were pink, although they were a shade darker than her outfit and a perfect match for the long-sleeved shirt he wore.

When the announcer boomed Blake's name through the loudspeaker, Donna reached over and laced her fingers through Jamie's. "Here we go. I'm pulling for our boys to have a good day. It's nice they keep drawing the same day to compete."

Jamie's heart expanded until he thought his ribs might break. Donna sincerely wanted Blake to do well in today's tie-down roping event. Her enthusiasm matched Jamie's. Why did it surprise him? He was pulling for Dustin, too. He'd already asked God's forgiveness for envying Dustin's circumstances that enabled him to travel to more rodeos than Blake.

Blake gave a nod and both Jamie and Donna stood. Blake's horse burst through the opening. Jamie winced. Had it been seconds too soon? He looked to the judges. No indication of a penalty so Blake didn't break the barrier. The loop went up and out, the calf went down, Blake dismounted and in nine seconds his hands were in the air.

"Well, folks, you just witnessed today's leader with a nine second tie-down. Let's give it up for Blake Martin." The loudspeakers boomed the announcer's voice across the large arena.

Donna let go of Jamie's hand, inserted her pinkies into the corners of her lips and blew a shrill whistle while Jamie clapped hard.

The next cowboy out of the chute was Grady Hawthorne. Jamie paid close attention to the cowboy's horse.

He hated to think the worst of a cowboy. Grady's horse fit all the signs of doping, and Grady kept to himself. When he was in a crowd, he seemed on edge with wary eyes always assessing the situation around him.

Grady and his horse's performance rang true with every other tie-down event he'd competed in at the Daddy of 'em All. His time of ten seconds even put him in at second for the day.

The crowd cheered. Jamie noticed Grady wasn't pleased with the time called. He whipped his hat from his head and beat it against his leg before grabbing the reins and mounting his horse. He set his mouth in a grim line and narrowed his eyes as he rode out of the arena.

The next two competitors earned decent scores, but they weren't a threat to either Blake or Grady.

"Dustin's up." Donna crossed her fingers.

"Let's hope his ride is as good as Blake's was." Jamie stretched his neck and watched Dustin back his horse into the correct stance. He gave a nod and before his horse took a step toward the barrier, his ride was stopped.

"We have a stubborn calf today who doesn't want to leave for work. This cowboy gets a do-over." The announcer made light of the calf trying to lie down in the chute.

"Oh, I hope this doesn't mess with Dustin's psyche." Donna leaned toward Jamie, nudging his shoulder.

"I'm sure it won't. He's a professional." Jamie wrapped an arm around Donna and squeezed. Her gardenia perfume tickled his nose and stirred memories of their kiss on top of the Ferris wheel. A thrill looped through Jamie. He and Donna needed to talk. He wanted her to know he was serious about this relationship. He'd lost her once and didn't plan to have a repeat performance. You only got one second chance.

"He's ready." Donna breathed the words as Dustin gave a nod.

The chute sprang open and a black-and-white calf raced out with Dustin's horse hot on its heels and Dustin's lasso spinning through the air. In seconds, the calf was roped.

"That didn't take long." Jamie watched Dustin's lanky frame run down the rope.

"He's going to have a good time." Donna answered with her eyes riveted on her nephew's performance.

Jamie leaned sideways and dropped his arm from Donna's shoulders when her arms lifted in unison with Dustin's hands. Eye's rounded, Donna turned to him. "What do you think?"

"Under ten seconds. The calf didn't get far out of the chute."

"Nine point three seconds. Dustin Blake moves into second place."

Jamie winced at Donna's shrill whistles and leaned his ear away while he clapped and stomped on the floor of the bleachers.

When the crowd settled down, Jamie looked at Donna. Bright happiness etched every line time had implanted on her features. She was more beautiful now than she was twenty years ago. He reached up and tucked a stray lock of hair behind her ear, reveling in its silkiness. Regret stung his heart. He'd missed watching the years and maturity paint a new picture on her features. Something he wouldn't let happen again.

"We have a couple of winners." Pride glowed in her eyes.

"Yes, we do." Jamie pulled her into a side embrace

and kissed her forehead. "I know it means missing the rest of the events, but let's go find the boys and congratulate them."

"Okay."

Jamie held Donna's hand and led her down the bleachers' stairs. Jamie listened to the announcers play-by-play of the next tie-downs. Blake and Dustin still held first and second place. When Jamie came to the gated entrance for the rodeo competitors he stopped and took out his cell phone.

"Grant's on duty today. I'll text him to come and let us in."

Jamie's phone jingled. "He'll be right here. He says there's trouble with Blake's and Dustin's ride."

Concern washed over Donna's face. "They called it fair. No one broke the barrier."

She started to shift her weight from one foot to the other. Jamie felt antsy too. Their rides had looked good.

Red-faced, Grant reached the gate, spoke to the guard on duty and waited for Donna and Jamie to walk through.

"What's going on?"

"Grady Hawthorne is making some loud accusations about your nephews." Grant cut a path with his hefty frame through the pens to the area housing the horse trailers.

A group of cowboys formed a circle. Jamie kept his grip tight on Donna's hand and pushed hard to break through the ring of onlookers.

Blake and Dustin stood side by side. One of the rodeo board members posted himself between them and Grady.

"I don't care. Nobody gets those scores naturally. I think they doped their horses. This one." Grady pointed to Dustin. "Could cover it up easily with his uncle being a stock contractor." He threw his hands in the air. "Maybe they're drugged up too, and that's why they're moving faster today."

Anger roared inside of Jamie. He fisted his hands. Grady was accusing Blake and Dustin of the exact thing Jamie suspected Grady was doing. Was Grady trying to throw people off his own scent? No cowboy could be this sore a loser. Not even Grady, a cowboy with a chip on this shoulder the size of Wyoming.

Blake's and Dustin's features twisted from confusion to anger.

"Why you—" Dustin stepped forward.

Blake caught his raised fist and stopped his swing. "Getting mad only makes us look guilty. We know we're innocent."

Witnessing Blake's calm demeanor tamped out some of Jamie's flames of anger. His nephew had a level head and even temper, something he didn't inherit from Jamie.

Jamie, Donna and Grant made their way to Dustin's and Blake's side. The board member talked to Grady in a firm tone and pointed in the direction of the exit. When Grady cleared the area, the board member turned on his heel and approached the small group.

"I'm sorry, boys. I don't believe Mr. Hawthorne. We'll have to do a full vet exam on your horses to prove him wrong. Grant, since it's obvious you know these boys, we can't use your services. I'll call you both with specifics later."

Jamie cocked a brow at Grant and gave a slight jerk with his head. Grant answered with a slight nod, bid everyone farewell and walked off in the same direction Grady had gone.

* * *

"I know we had plans to tour the Old West Museum today." Donna sighed. "After this incident, I don't know if I'm up to it."

Grady Hawthorne's accusations irritated her, especially after she defended him yesterday to Jamie. She recognized a loneliness in his eyes. Was it the reason why he pushed people away on purpose? Was he his own worst enemy?

Jamie cupped his palm over her cheek. "We know those accusations are false and so do our nephews."

Donna held her breath, wanting Jamie to reassure her with a tender kiss.

"Get your hands off my sister," Cameron growled.

Her heart turned to lead and dropped to her stomach.

"I told you the other night, it's Donna's decision not yours." Jamie patted his palm against Donna's cheek before removing his hand.

Cameron planted himself in front of Donna. His eyes bore into hers. "How many times do I have to tell you, you can't trust Jamie Martin?"

"That is enough, Cameron. I've been an adult for a long time and I can make my own decisions. Is there something special you want or did you come over to cause more trouble?" Donna inched closer to Jamie, their arms brushing.

"I stumbled across you making a fool of yourself while I was trying to find Dustin. I thought I'd go with him to the board office." Cameron angled his body sideways so Jamie faced his back. "I take it you know what happened."

"I saw and heard most of it." Donna nodded. "Dustin headed toward his horse trailer." She pointed toward the area, hating to sic Cameron on Dustin. She just didn't have the strength to deal with her brother right now.

Cameron stalked off without a goodbye and Donna released a cleansing breath. "I want to sit down and sip a cool drink while I process what happened."

"Sounds good. Grant keeps a cooler in his truck. He has chairs, too. It will be closer than the concessions."

"Lead the way."

When they reached Grant's veterinary truck, Jamie unlocked the cab with the spare key Grant gave him and pulled two canvas bags from the storage area behind the front seat of the cab. He pulled a chair out of the bag, unfolded it and placed it on the ground for Donna. "Probably not the most comfortable."

"I'm past the point of being fussy." She sat down in the taunt canvas seat and watched Jamie repeat the process.

"And now." Jamie turned back into the open cab door and flicked the top off a cooler. "We have sweet tea or lemonade."

"Lemonade." Donna watched him pull two individual bottles out of the cooler and replace the lid. He handed her a bottle. She swiped at the water trickling down the plastic bottle before twisting off the lid.

Jamie eased into his chair. "Dustin has three horses he uses for his tie-down events, doesn't he?"

Nodding, Donna swallowed the tart lemonade. "Yes. Their hired men meet him at the rodeos. They switch out horses so his animals can get a rest. He's actually in the market for a fourth horse."

"Humph." Jamie gave a small snort. "Did he switch them out at this rodeo?" Jamie lifted his bottle to his lips.

Donna frowned. "Yes. Why?"

"Mid-rodeo events? I thought the horse he rode the first day was dappled. Today's was chestnut."

"Yes, those are two of his horses. What are you getting at?" she asked, the sternness inflected in her question intentional. There were no rules against it. What was Jamie fishing for?

"Nothing. I was wondering. I'm not as young as I used to be and I was sure he rode a different colored horse earlier in the week." Jamie took another sip of his drink and stared off into the distance rather than meeting Donna's gaze.

Donna pursed her lips. Jamie hadn't seemed to notice her clipped words and his answer was nonchalant with no defensiveness. By his stance, he appeared to be pondering something. Maybe wishing Blake had the same advantage? Donna relaxed and took a drink of the cool tangy lemonade. The events of the day must be taking more of a toll than she thought.

"Let's say a prayer for the boys." Jamie clasped his hand over hers where it rested on the chair's armrest.

"Sure." Donna bowed her head.

"Heavenly Father, please look down upon Blake and Dustin. Give them strength during this difficulty in their careers. Help them to feel Your wondrous love and the love of their families. Amen."

She lifted her head and looked at him. "Jamie, will you stop by my trailer tonight after Cowboy Church? We can pick up some ice cream and have dessert under the stars." Immediate heat crept up her neck and warmed her cheeks. How had she made eating ice cream sound so romantic and intimate? She hadn't meant to, had she?

"Hmm...sounds great. I can't though. Grant and I have something to take care of tonight. Can I take a rain check?" Jamie turned his eyes on her and flashed a sincere smile.

Insecurity rushed through her. She broke eye contact and dropped her gaze to her chest. Her emotional reaction to Jamie had made her feel feminine and forget all of her inadequacies for a while. But now they came rushing back. If he knew the truth about her, would he want her?

Twenty years ago, Jamie had openly appreciated the physical attributes of women. So far, though, she hadn't noticed his eyes roving once. If he knew her body was altered, scarred, would that change?

"Sure, we can postpone it until tomorrow night. It can be our last hurrah before going our separate ways." *Again.*

Jamie squeezed her hand. "I don't want to go our separate ways. I know we haven't really discussed it. I want a relationship with you that ends with us building a life together. I know we have some hurdles to jump before it happens. Donna, I love you. I always have and I always will."

Happiness zinged through Donna. It was too much to hold, and spilled from her eyes. She'd missed hearing Jamie's smooth baritone say those three simple words. "I love you, too." Her admission floated out on a soft sigh.

Jamie's wide smile brought out one of her own.

"The first hurdle we have to get over is putting the past behind us. I need to know you've forgiven me for the all the pain and tribulation I caused your family. And not to fulfill my sobriety step either. We need to start out fresh. Do you agree?"

Start out fresh meant she had to tell him about her lumpectomy. Fear drummed her heart, its vibrations

dulled her hearing. She surveyed the area. A few cowboys were scattered about, but none within hearing distance. She knew this conversation could alter her future
the way the surgery had altered her body.

*Therefore if anyone is in Christ, he is a new creation;
the old has gone, the new has come!*

The remembered scripture reassured her this was
the right time to have this conversation.

"Jamie, there is something I need to tell you. Something you need to consider before we go any further in
our relationship."

Jamie sat at attention and leaned forward.

Licking her lips, Donna started to open her mouth.
Antsy, she pushed from her chair. She paced over to the
compartment of Grant's truck. Drawing a deep breath,
she turned. "Jamie, I'm not the woman I once was."

Chapter 11

Emotions reared up and kicked at her heart like a bucking horse's hooves ate up the arena dirt. Her breathing became rapid. A moist sheen covered her eyes. Other than her family and a few girlfriends, no one else knew her secret.

Jamie's eyes went wide, then narrowed when he furrowed his brow. His gaze roved over her body, resting on her face. He stood. "We're both older, Donna. Twenty years of gravity has changed us both."

Donna fisted her hands, then released them. This was hard and he wasn't making it any easier, thinking her problem lay in the fact she was no longer the youthful image advertising companies pushed on society. In fact, at forty-four, she thought she'd held up well with the exception of the lumpectomy. She took a step toward Jamie.

"It's not about the ravages of age." Donna gave her

head a shake, blinking rapidly and failing to hold back a tear. The warm liquid traced a path down the side of her face.

Two quick steps and Jamie faced her. He brushed the tear off her cheek with the pad of his thumb. "What is it?" He frowned. The parenthesis lines around his mouth deepened. He placed his hands on her arms below her shoulders and stared deeply into her eyes. "Tell me."

Finding strength from the trust in his eyes, she cleared her throat. "Over a year ago, when I had my first mammogram."

Sadness forced the concern from Jamie's features and brought a lump of emotion to Donna's throat. Closing her eyes, she swallowed hard. Could she go on? She didn't want to open her eyes and find pity shining from Jamie's hazel irises.

"Donna, did you have cancer? Do you have cancer?"

Fear graveled Jamie's voice. She needed to tell him. Heart pattering, ears thundering, Donna slowly opened her eyes and nodded. "I've had a lumpectomy." She hadn't realized she'd lifted a hand until she felt its weight on her chest. She patted the area where her hand rested. "I'll understand if…" Her voice shook and trailed off.

Jamie's hands released her arms.

He didn't want damaged goods. Hot tears burned her eyes and a sob formed in her throat.

Then in an instant she was wrapped in a tight, loving embrace.

"I'm so sorry you had to go through that." Jamie's whisper tickled her cheek, his voice, low and husky, laced with emotion.

Donna buried her face in his neck and wrapped her arms around him.

After a few minutes, Jamie pulled her to arm's length. "I want you to know it doesn't matter to me."

Love shone in his eyes.

"Are you sure?" She needed to know. She was ready to forgive him and give her heart to him.

"I've found you again and I'm never letting you go." Jamie pulled her to him and lowered his head.

Her heart spun circles in her chest when his lips met hers. The emotion in his kiss weakened her knees. He ended the kiss and stared into her eyes.

"Are you convinced I mean it?" Jamie's lips curved into the cocky grin of his youth.

"Oh, yeah." Donna laughed, releasing her tension. She rested her head on Jamie's shoulder.

"We're going to figure this out." Jamie leaned against the truck, pulling Donna with him.

"Are you sure you don't want to eat ice cream under the stars tonight? It could be our own private celebration of reuniting." Donna lifted her head to drink in Jamie's handsome features.

"I can't."

"Come on, what could be more important than a romantic evening?" she said teasingly.

"Unfortunately, there is something." The plains of Jamie's face turned serious.

"What is it?"

"It doesn't concern you."

"Jamie, if we are going to move forward with our relationship we need to trust and confide in each other. I can tell by your face whatever this is, it's troubling you." Donna reached up and rubbed the bristly stubble on his cheek.

"Everything you're saying is true. However, in my

pastoral duties, there are some things I'll never be able to share with you."

She looked up at him. "I understand. I'll send up prayers for your unspoken concern."

"I'd appreciate it." Jamie pulled her into a tight hug.

Donna sighed. Jamie's embrace was a safe place she never wanted to leave again.

Donna spent the late afternoon wandering through Frontier Park. Alone. She knew it was selfish to feel miffed at Jamie when he felt something else was more important than spending time with her. They'd wasted so many years not being together, she wanted to spend every possible moment with him. And it didn't seem hard for Jamie to join Grant and walk away, leaving her to her own devices for the rest of the day and evening.

She glanced at her watch. It was finally time for her to head over to the Cowboy Church tent and prepare for the evening worship service and see Jamie. Happiness lifted her heart at the thought, chasing away the afternoon's blues. Donna made a beeline for the FCC tent.

When she arrived Jamie was deep in conversation with a young man. The young cowboy gave a nod and two heads bowed, the brim of their Stetson's touching. Sheepishness crept through Donna. She chided herself for her earlier feelings. Leading people to God and helping them ease their burdens trumped strolling through the fairground atmosphere hand in hand with her. Didn't it?

Silently, she walked to the portable keyboard and readied it for the service. Adjusting the volume she played a few hymns while people gathered. Grant's usual chair in the front row sat empty. This was the first time he had missed a service when Jamie delivered the sermon. Maybe there was a veterinary emergency.

Jamie preached an inspiring lesson. Donna marveled at the way he spoke from his heart, never reading from a prewritten sermon. So engrossed in his message, Donna missed her cue for the closing hymn until Jamie turned to her and flashed a smile.

After shaking hands with all of the people on their way out, Jamie came over to Donna and pecked a kiss on her cheek.

"Do you need me to give you a lift back to your camper?"

"No. Cameron said he'd take me back." Donna purposely kept her voice light. She knew Cameron would lecture all the back to the RV, and her heart wanted Jamie to take her home.

She caught Jamie's slight wince at the mention of Cameron's name. Would it change his mind? Would he find the time to drive her to the RV park?

He released a deep sigh. Hope threaded through her at the possibility of a romantic evening with Jamie and her chance to forgive him.

Jamie rubbed his chin with his thumb and forefinger. "Will you be leaving soon?"

Donna furrowed her brow at Jamie's odd question. "He has some things to finish up with the animals' care and then we'll be on our way."

Relief washed across Jamie's face. "Okay, I'll see you in the morning then."

Jamie's stance was off. He shifted his weight from one foot to the other. Instead of staring straight into her eyes, his gaze seemed to dart around the tent. All character traits from his past. Suspicion whirled through

Donna and she failed to keep it out of her voice. "Okay, I'll see you in the morning."

What was causing Jamie's uneasiness? The mention of Cameron's name or the situation he couldn't tell her about?

Jamie hated not being honest with Donna, but it was for her own good. He didn't want her dragged into a scandal, if there was one. Jamie knew Blake didn't dope his horse or take drugs himself. Not only was it against Blake's principles, his budget wouldn't support the expense of drug use for either animal or human. A grin came to Jamie's lips. He'd never known such a fiscally responsible young person as Blake.

When the grimness of the situation settled back on his mind, the corners of his mouth eased into a firm line. Some of what Grady said could be true about Dustin. He switched horses and could be assisted by Cameron. But Jamie really didn't think so. He and Grant had spent the afternoon sizing up the situation and trailing behind Grady.

Grady owned the same make and model rig Blake did, so Jamie knew there were sleeping quarters in the front. Grady remained on-site with his horse all night, unlike Blake and Dustin who boarded their horses for this rodeo and spent the night elsewhere. It would be easy for a troublemaker to make good on his accusations.

Jamie scanned the area for Grant. He spotted him sitting in a lawn chair in the shade thrown on the ground by the vet's box on his pickup.

Lord, forgive me of my suspicions. Prove to me this cowboy was sputtering accusations in angry frustration. Help him realize there is more to life than winning, and if it's financial burdens making him lash out at his peers, please ease those burdens for him. Help him to know and trust You with his life. Amen.

"How's it going?" Jamie clapped a hand on Grant's shoulder.

"Not much to report. Dustin's horse is penned with Cameron's stock. Grady keeps his tied by his trailer unless he takes off for a while. Then he loads it into the trailer."

"Any sign of foul play?"

"No. A couple of rough-looking cowboys stopped and talked to Grady for a while. It didn't appear anything changed hands."

"It doesn't mean he doesn't have drugs with him or didn't hire them to drug Blake's and Dustin's horses."

"True. He does feed his horse pellets. I watched him dump some into a bucket."

Jamie squatted down behind Grant, lowering his voice. "Were you able to draw a vile of blood?"

"Yes. I don't feel right about sneaking around to do it either."

"But if he is doping his horse and thinks it will need a physical, too, he'll stop. And we can't make accusations without proof."

"I know. I got the sample from Blake's horse, too, so we only need to get some from Dustin's horse. Cameron sticks pretty close to his stock though."

"He's leaving soon to take Donna back to the RV park. It should be dark soon and we can head over to the pen. Have you tested the other two?"

"No, I'm waiting to run the tests on all three blood samples. I want to take my time so everything is accurate if we're showing them to the board in the morning."

Jamie nodded and rubbed his chin. He wished he was

sitting beside Donna under the stars sharing ice cream and planning their future. Tomorrow this would be over and he could be honest with her.

Grant stood. "Take this chair. I'm going to rest my eyes in the pickup. I think it's going to be a long night."

Jamie agreed.

When Donna's phone finally zinged, she unlocked the screen and read Cameron's message. She'd been sitting on a bench people watching for the last hour waiting for Cameron to finish whatever it was he was doing. I'm ready to haul you to your camper. Meet me in the stock area.

Huffing, Donna tucked her phone into her purse. Hauling her? She wasn't livestock. She was his sister. Jamie was right. Cameron didn't respect her. She'd use this irritation at her brother to fuel her courage to tell him she planned to continue her renewed relationship with Jamie, declare her love and warn Cameron he'd better find the same forgiveness in his heart.

The night air held a chill and clouds covered a full moon. It didn't stop Donna from deliberately strolling to the stock area of Frontier Park. The closer she drew to the penned area, the less frequent the overhead light became and the more pungent the smell of the animals.

She stopped when her phone jangled. Cameron's text told her he was waiting in his pickup in the parking lot. She rolled her eyes at her brother's impatience. She'd need to turn around. Movement close to the pens caught her eye. Straining to see through the pens bars and the night shadows, Donna saw two forms wearing cowboy hats zigzagging through the fencing toward her brother's livestock.

Grasping her cell phone in her hands, Donna walked

closer to the pens, inching along the side parallel to the men. A few horses sensed people and snorted. Were these men some of the Greenes' hired hands? If they were, why was their stance hunched and sneaky?

The cowboys stopped and stared into the pen housing their championship bull. Donna turned her back to the men so she could shield the light of her smart phone and flicked the screen until she found her camera. She might need to get a picture of whatever they were up to.

Warm air blew on her neck. She squeaked but managed to stop her scream. Had they seen her while she prepped her cell phone? Heart palpitating at a high rate of speed, Donna slowly turned her head and looked into a big brown eye. Her heart dropped. She placed a hand to her chest.

Silly horse, your curiosity startled me. Donna patted the horse's nose before she stepped away from the pen and crept closer to the two men staring intently at Antagonist.

Her brother tried her nerves, but it didn't mean she wanted to see him disappointed again. She couldn't let any harm come to this championship bull. Antagonist was going to the National Finals Rodeo.

With each of her silent steps, the hazy shapes of the cowboys took form. One wore a dark felt hat. The other a straw hat. Donna stopped by the corner of fencing and strained to see into the darkness. The men's builds were familiar. She blinked, then blinked again.

It was Jamie and Grant. Relief washed through her. She took a step toward them, ready to say hello. It was obvious Jamie's pastor duties were over and he was helping Grant check the animals.

Donna slipped her cell phone into her purse. There was no need to take a picture. She turned and wound back through the maze of the stock pens to find the path Jamie and Grant had taken.

It would be nice to have Jamie with her when she talked to Cameron about her decision to forgive Jamie and begin a relationship with him. Maybe Grant could come, too. A unified front would certainly help the situation and maybe help keep tempers in check. Donna knew her brother and Jamie. She wasn't naive. This conversation would include anger and terse words.

She rounded the corner of a pen close to the men. The cloud cover broke. Moonlight glowed through the darkness. Jamie had climbed onto the fencing. Grant lifted his hand.

Donna stopped in her tracks. She didn't want to believe it. She'd been around animals her entire life and there was no mistaking what Grant held. A syringe. She stepped back into a horse's shadow.

Old hurt wound through her. Had Jamie played her for a fool? Gaining her trust until she told him Cameron's evening schedule? Cameron's words of warning about Jamie sounded in her head. She should call Cameron. No, it'd take him a few minutes to get back to this area from the parking lot. Those few minutes might cost the Greene family another chance at having a bull in the National Finals Rodeo.

It was up to her. Heart racing, she stepped out into the moonlight.

"What are you planning to do to Antagonist?"

Chapter 12

Both men's bodies jerked. Jamie jumped from the fencing and Grant spun around on the heel of his boot. In the moonlight's glow, she saw guilt chiseled into Jamie's features.

"Donna, you about scared me to death."

Jamie's scolding tone looped through her and cinched her anger tight, making her as furious as a bull in a chute.

"Me, too." Grant shook his head and put his hands behind his back.

Donna cringed at the smooth evenness of Jamie's voice. His tone pulled her back to the past. She'd heard it many times before when he tried to cover for his indiscretions. She quirked a brow. "What are you doing here?"

Jamie stepped toward her and stopped directly in front of her, blocking her view of Grant.

He wasn't getting by with lying to her again. "I don't

believe you've answered my question." She folded her arms over her chest and stared directly into his hazel irises, knowing they reflected a fool. She'd fallen, hook, line and sinker. She hugged her arms tighter, cringing yet again. She'd revealed her secret. She'd been a vulnerable middle-aged fool, thinking a man would want her in this condition.

Moisture sheened her eyes. *Don't cry.* Her command did no good, her tears welled.

"Oh, Donna." Tenderness half-lidded Jamie's eyes. He reached for her. She backed away.

"Are you sabotaging our bull? Again?"

"No, Donna, we aren't." Hurt sagged every feature on Jamie's face. "This is not what you think."

"Right. You're slinking through the pen with a veterinarian holding a syringe filled with who knows what."

Jamie grabbed her shoulders.

She jerked hard freeing them.

"I can't tell you. I don't want you to be involved." The pleading look in his eyes softened her heart, made her want to hear him out.

You can't trust him. You're not honoring Dad's memory. Cameron's words rippled through her mind. Donna squeezed her eyes shut to help fortify herself against Jamie's charms. Opening her eyes, Donna took a step closer to Jamie. "It's too late. I'm here." She spoke through clenched teeth.

The animals penned beside them began to rustle.

Jamie glanced over his shoulder at Grant, then turned to Donna. "I need you to trust me." He dipped his head unable to look her in the eyes.

"I need you to tell me."

"I'm not going to." Jamie grabbed her shoulders,

tighter than before. "There are some things you don't need to know about."

Donna tried to jerk free. Jamie's grip was too strong. "Like picking up rodeo queens, wrecking a company vehicle, killing a prized bull and almost my brother?" Donna words galloped out before she could stop them. "And to think I almost forgave you."

Leaning her head close to Jamie's, Donna sniffed the air.

Jamie's eyes widened. He released his hold and staggered back. Had she smelled alcohol? It was hard to tell. The area was pungent with the smell of animals. She hoped her words pierced Jamie's heart like the needle Grant held would have pierced Antagonist's hide had she not shown up. She needed to get the syringe away from Grant. Donna took a step and looked past Jamie.

Grant was gone.

Everything that happened minutes ago ran in slow motion through Jamie's mind until the darkness swallowed up Donna's retreating image, then real time began. Had she said she was calling Cameron? Going to find Cameron?

Either way it didn't matter. He and Grant needed to draw blood from Dustin's horse to prove to the board Grady Hawthorne's accusations were false.

"Where are you?" Jamie turned and whispered into the darkness.

"Over here."

A cloud moved and covered the light of the moon. Jamie squinted, then he heard the fencing rattle and walked in the direction of the noise.

"Did you get a sample?" His hushed tone made him sound as sneaky and guilty as Donna thought he was.

His heart squeezed so hard he almost doubled over. She'd tried to smell his breath. His breathing became ragged. Hurt pinched every nerve in his body.

"Yes. You all right?"

Jamie gave his head a shake.

"Do you want a drink?"

It sounded like an offer, but Jamie knew it wasn't. He wiped a hand across his mouth. "Every day I want a drink more than anything else." Jamie paused and looked in the direction Donna had fled. "Until now. Now I want Donna's love more than anything."

Jamie turned his eyes to Grant. Emotion hitched his voice. "But I think I just lost her trust and her love."

"Where are you?" Cameron's gruff voice boomed over the cell phone.

Donna ran toward the parking lot. Her panted breath burned her lungs. "Cameron, listen to me. I caught Jamie and Grant messing around Antagonist's pen." Her pace slowed. Running made her gasp for breath. It was impossible for her to talk on the phone. "That's why I called you." She huffed and stopped when she reached the area she thought he'd parked his truck in. "I'm here in the parking lot. Where are you?"

She peered into the darkness at the shadowy vehicles scattered throughout the lot.

Gears ground to her far left. Headlights popped on and illuminated the area. Donna hit End on her phone and waved her arms in the air. Cameron pulled the pickup alongside of her. She reached for the door handle and stepped up on the running board.

"Hold it." Cameron rounded the cab of the truck. She saw the fury on his face when he walked through the headlights' glow.

Donna stepped down. The passenger door opened and Dustin slid out.

"What exactly did you see?" Cameron's terseness bristled the hair on the back of her neck.

"Grant and Jamie were sneaking around the animal pens. I followed them to see what they were doing. When a cloud moved, I saw a syringe in Grant's hand." Donna's words huffed out between pants. Her head and heart pounded in unison. She lifted a hand and rubbed her temple while she tried to catch her breath.

"And." Cameron's bellow echoed through the parking lot.

"Let her catch her breath." Dustin put an arm around her shoulder.

"I asked what they were doing. Jamie wouldn't tell me. While we were arguing—" Donna winced knowing what Cameron's reaction would be. She put a fist to her lips and looked at her brother. "Grant disappeared."

Cameron kicked at nothing and threw up his hands. "I told you to stay away from him. Get in the truck and wait until Dustin and I get back."

Donna obliged her brother. She rested her forehead against the cool window glass in the door and watched the men's shadows fade into the darkness. The pop chug of the diesel engine ticked away at her mind like a clock counting off minutes. She began to rewind and play back the events of the week.

Had she become one of those lonely women who let a man snooker them? A tear spilled from her eye and trickled down her cheek. At least Jamie had only taken her heart and not her fortune. She gave a small snort. He had taken their fortune long ago. Her dad had borrowed money against the promise of Old Dependable. To make matters worse, the insurance papers on their champion stock hadn't been processed either. They'd lost everything except their home.

Donna rubbed the spot between her eyes trying to alleviate the pounding in her head. Why hadn't she listened to Cameron? Her brother worked so hard to get their stock company back on track. He even took a night job at a grocery store chain stocking shelves. How he managed to work beside their dad from sun up to suppertime, then head to town and work most the night, Donna didn't know. All she knew was that all of the money he made at the second job he put back into the family business.

She truly hadn't appreciated it; she'd been so heartbroken over Jamie.

Scanning the area, Donna hoped she'd see Cameron and Dustin emerge from the shadows. Had they found Jamie and Grant? Or worse, a drugged bull?

"God, why is this happening?" Anguished, Donna covered her face with her hands and sobbed. Her tears stopped with the realization she'd repeated the same plea over a year ago when the doctor diagnosed her cancer. Had she not grown at all as a Christian? Why was she trying to deal with the turmoil of the situation on her own?

Donna closed her eyes, folded her hands and began to commune with God.

The crack of the door hinge releasing forced Donna to say *Amen*. Dustin slid behind the wheel of the truck. The dim dash lights revealed no emotion on his face.

"Well?"

Dustin shrugged. "We couldn't find them. Uncle Cameron is spitting mad, though. Better slide over and give him some room."

Donna yielded to Dustin's suggestion in the nick of

time. Cameron threw open the door and slammed his frame onto the passenger seat.

"Let's go." He commanded Dustin with his eyes riveted out the windshield.

Dustin put the truck into gear and eased it through the parking lot.

Cameron's anger thickened the air, making it stifling. Donna tensed her body, trying to make it smaller and steady to avoid bumping into Cameron on the turns.

"I don't know why you don't listen to me." Cameron bit out the words. Donna braced herself.

"This isn't my fault." Donna gulped. Neither was the accident in the past, but deep down she knew Cameron resented her for it.

"Yes, it is. You invited trouble back into your life, which in turn invited trouble back into *my* life."

Cameron pounded a fist on the dash. Donna jumped. "History is not going to repeat itself. My bull is going to the National Finals."

"Uncle Cameron, we didn't find any evidence they messed with Antagonist. He was still upright and eating. His eyes looked okay." Dustin turned in the opposite direction of Donna's campground.

"Listen, you. You were born with a Bliss-monogrammed silver spoon in your mouth. You don't know what it's like to struggle and work hard for everything. Everything you've ever wanted you've gotten handed to you."

Donna reared back in the seat to avoid getting poked with the finger Cameron jabbed in Dustin's direction.

"Right." Dustin huffed out the word in a sarcastic tone.

"Cameron, lay off him. Not only is he family, none of this is his fault. Did you call a vet to check out our bull?"

"Our bull?" Cameron's eyes bugged when he looked at Donna.

She cut him off before he could continue. "Yes, our bull. You know Deanne and I have a stake in the family business, too. You may run it, but it belongs to all of us."

Cameron's face twisted in anger and Donna was certain hers mirrored his.

"I think you both need to calm down." Dustin's words drawled through the tension in the pickup cab. "We have enough to deal with, without a family quarrel."

Donna's shoulders sagged. "You're right. Cameron, I'm sorry to take my anger and frustration with this day out on you." Although her sibling did try her nerves, it was Jamie's actions that had her riled up. And Grady Hawthorne's accusations. Maybe Grady, Grant and Jamie were working together on this scheme.

The twist of Donna's heart brought fresh moisture to her eyes. She was such a fool.

"Being sorry won't save our bacon if something happens to Antagonist. I told you to not to associate with Jamie Martin." Cameron's tone never lost its hard edge.

Donna knew an apology would never come.

Dustin slowed the truck and turned into the parking lot of a hotel. Donna had been so busy bickering, she hadn't paid any attention to her surroundings.

"Out," Dustin said as he pulled under the carport of the establishment.

"But this is my vehicle."

"Yeah, and mine is still on the grounds of Frontier Park. "I'll be back to get you in the morning. Or better yet, you can hitch a ride with one of your buddies tomorrow."

Cameron glowered at Dustin. "You're not taking my truck."

"How else is Donna going to get back to the camp-grounds? I believe it was your idea for the three of us to share two vehicles. Now, get out."

Donna couldn't help it. She turned and looked at her nephew with nothing short of awe. She knew he didn't see her, his eyes were focused on Cameron.

After a few tense seconds, the door latch popped and Cameron exited the cab, slamming the door behind him. Donna unbuckled, slid to the passenger seat and pulled the seat belt across her chest, securing it in the lock.

"Wow. You're all grown-up." Donna reached over and gave Dustin's biceps a playful punch.

The corners of his mouth twitched and he turned the dual-wheeler back onto the street. "Why is he so disre-spectful to everyone? I know he's struggled. I can't help it if oil runs under our land. And you." Dustin shook his head. "He is mean to you, Aunt Donna."

Donna sighed. "He never used to be before the ac-cident. Things changed afterward. I suppose it goes back to me dating Jamie. If I hadn't been in a relation-ship with him, the tragedy wouldn't have happened."

She splayed the fingers of her left hand. Even though she'd given Jamie's diamond back, her mind's eye saw the tear-shaped diamond set in white gold. She'd loved the ring. She'd loved the man. Years ago she'd ignored his flaws, chalking it up to youth. What was her ex-cuse this time?

Foolishness washed through her.

"I plan to stay the night at your place. You know, in case you get an unwanted visitor."

"You don't plan to retaliate, do you?"

"No, I don't. Blake's an upstanding cowboy. He wouldn't want to win the rodeo by cheating. He speaks highly of his uncle so…" Dustin's voice trailed off.

Donna turned and looked at her nephew. "So?"

"Promise not to get mad at me?"

Donna nodded.

"I don't think Jamie would do something bad like drugging an animal."

"You don't know him the way I do."

"That's true, I don't. I do know he runs a ranch for..."

"Retired and injured rodeo stock." Donna finished Dustin's sentence.

"Does that sound like someone who'd intentionally hurt your bull?"

"No." Donna sighed. "No, it doesn't." Why had she jumped to conclusions? He'd asked her to trust him and she hadn't. Shame filled her heart.

"He loves you." Dustin's voice turned soft.

She didn't deserve it. Not after this.

"I can see it in his eyes. And you love him, too, don't you?"

"For the last twenty years." A strange sensation filled Donna at her admission, peace. It was the first time she'd said the words out loud, although she'd thought them many times over the years. "I was hurt Jamie was with that rodeo queen. Although I never doubted his love for me, he had a wandering eye. He told me nothing happened or nothing he could remember. Your grandpa and Cameron pressured me to give Jamie's ring back. In the heat of the moment, I did and told him I didn't want to see him anymore."

"Did you miss him?"

Donna didn't miss the wistfulness in Dustin's voice. Was this Casanova really a romantic at heart? "Terribly. And I knew if I saw him, I'd forgive him." *Just like now.* "So I stopped going to rodeos. This probably is my fault. I should have stayed away."

"No, you shouldn't have. It means a lot to me to have you here. Besides, Aunt Donna, you deserve to be happy. I want you to know if Jamie makes you happy don't even consider what your family thinks. Go for it."

Dustin pulled the pickup into the parking spot beside her camper.

Both of them surveyed the neighboring RV. A soft light, like the illumination of a television, glowed through the living room window.

"Think he's over there?" She said the words without even thinking.

"I know he is. He's peeking out the bedroom window."

Hurt and regret had gnawed at Jamie for the past two days and worked up a powerful thirst. He was relieved Donna made it home safe and sound on Thursday night. The only glimpse of Donna he'd seen in the last forty-eight hours was when Cameron picked her up each morning. Jamie peered through his trailer window at Donna's dark camper. He wished she was home. He wished she was with him. He wished she wasn't angry.

He and Grant should never have stopped to admire Antagonist, which was a fine specimen of a Brahma bull. If they'd continued on their mission, none of this mess would have happened.

You should have been honest. The right thing to do was to ask both Dustin and Grady to let Grant draw a vile of blood from their horses for testing.

He'd been so certain Grady was making accusations to throw the scent on someone else's trail. After all, tomorrow was the final tie-down competition. If Blake and Dustin were disqualified, he'd win the Frontier

Days event, take the lead in points standing and qual-
ify for the National Finals Rodeo.

Boy, had Jamie been wrong. That wasn't what
Grant's testing found at all.

The purr of a pickup engine pulled Jamie from his
thoughts. He moved the corner of his bedroom curtain.
Like the past two nights, Dustin slid from behind the
wheel, opened the truck door for Donna and escorted
her into the camper.

Once a light came on, Jamie released the corner of
the curtain. He wanted to talk to her, explain. Yet he
knew Dustin was a barrier so he couldn't get close to
Donna. Besides he couldn't take seeing the distrust and
loathing in her eyes.

Jamie strode to the kitchen. So much for good in-
tentions. He was such a mess-up. He ran a glass full of
water and drank it down in one gulp, wishing it burned
down his throat and left a bitter taste in his mouth. He
closed his eyes and imagined the warmth of alcohol
washing over his body, relaxing his muscles, fuzzing
his feelings.

His mouth watered. He smacked his lips. His body
begged for the warm numbness to wash away his heartache. He began searching through cupboards. It didn't
matter if he was drunk or sober, he'd messed up with
Donna.

Slamming the cupboard door, Jamie stuffed his
hands in his front pockets. He fingered his sobriety
coin. If he lost Donna's love over this stupid stunt, the
coin was worthless. He flipped it onto the counter. It
was just another reminder of what a failure he had become.

Jamie grabbed his jacket from the chair and stuffed
his arms through it. He knew he didn't have what he

was looking for in his cupboards. Judging by the loud music and laughter throughout the campground, somebody did. Slipping out the door, Jamie walked to the street and headed toward the loudest party.

Chapter 13

Sunday morning Donna and Dustin walked side by side. She glanced over at her nephew and wondered if his insides were a bundle of nerves. Hers were. She'd slipped on jeans, her bandanna-print blouse and red cowboy boots. Now she wished she'd opted for lighter footwear. The boots seemed to have turned to lead weights and grew heavier with each step toward the board office.

Dustin exuded confidence that seemed both unshakable and unrealistic.

"Are you doing okay?" Donna stopped and waited for Dustin to open the entry door.

"Yeah. I know I'm not guilty. What's there to worry about?"

Donna's jaw dropped. "Only your career, points standing and reputation."

"I'm innocent of those accusations. I know it and God knows it, so I have nothing to worry about."

They walked down a short hall. Donna marveled at Dustin's trust in God. Would she ever get to that point in her relationship with her Lord? She hoped so.

Rounding a corner, Cameron came into sight. He leaned against the wall glowering at them as they walked toward him.

"No one else is here yet."

"We are early. The board doesn't convene for a few more minutes." Donna surveyed the area. No sign of Blake, Jamie or Grady.

Nerves twitched her stomach. Surely they were going to show up. Grady's accusations were serious. Movement caught Donna's eye as Blake rounded the corner. Surprise registered on his face as he looked at, then past, the Greene family. Had he expected his uncle to be here?

"'Morning." Dustin held out a hand and shook Blake's.

"Dustin." Blake extended his hand to Donna. "'Morning, ma'am."

Donna forced a smile, grasped Blake's hand and squeezed. His rough calluses a reminder of his hard work and what he and her nephew stood to lose. "I know everything will turn out all right." Her voice held steady and didn't betray the doubt whirling through her.

"I hope so." Blake glanced behind him before turning to Cameron. "Mr. Greene." He nodded and tipped his hat.

Cameron continued to stare at the opposite wall.

Donna tensed. Surely her brother could shake hands or acknowledge Blake. The young cowboy had done nothing to their family except be polite.

"Have any of you seen my uncle?"

Cameron snorted. Donna shot him a look.

"Nope." Dustin stuck his hands in his pockets.

"Sorry." Donna held up her palms and shrugged.

"He never came home last night." Worry covered Blake's features. "I've tried calling and texting. I get no answer."

"Maybe his cell phone battery died or he's not picking up a signal." Donna hoped her suggestions would ease Blake's worries. She also hoped they were true.

"I hope that's it." Blake unsnapped his shirt pocket and reached inside with two fingers. "I found this on the kitchen counter."

A small weathered token rested in Blake's palm.

Donna's gasp echoed down the hall. Blake's revelation passed his worry to Donna, infecting her like a bad flu virus.

This was serious. Donna lifted Jamie's sobriety coin from Blake's hand. Was she responsible? Her heart dropped to her stomach. She was. She'd seen the pleading in his eyes, then the hurt her angry words caused. She reeled with guilt and clasped Blake's hand harder to keep her balance. "We need to find him."

"I've been trying. Grant's not answering either."

"Did you check all the bars?" Cameron spat.

Blake's jaw dropped and his eyes misted before he hung his head. Donna seethed at Cameron's words. She spun around to face him. "Apologize at once."

"I will not." Cameron tugged on the waistband of his jeans and stood to his full height.

"Yes, you will." Dustin moved to Donna's side. "I don't agree with all your actions or attitudes, but you are still my uncle and I love you. That is exactly how Blake here feels about Jamie."

Cameron blew out his breath and pushed between

Donna and Dustin. "Look, son, I'm sorry. I shouldn't have said that. I can see you're upset."

Blake stole a quick glance at Donna before he met Cameron's stare. "You're forgiven."

The words had a strange effect on Cameron. He swayed and staggered backward as if Blake was an angry Brahma bull ready to charge. His features became contrite.

A door in the hallway opened. "Blake, Dustin are you ready?" The board member swung the door open wide. "Cameron and Donna you're welcome, too."

Donna took one last look down the hall. She reached for Blake's hand and gave it a reassuring squeeze when they walked through the door.

Just as they were ready to sit down, there was a rap on the already opened door. "Can we join this party?" Jamie's baritone boomed through the room.

Hat askew, Jamie stood with his thumbs looped through his belt loops. By the looks of his stained, wrinkled clothing, he'd spent the night in them. The signature cocksure grin of his youth revealed he felt relaxed and brave. The rest of his features looked haggard. Redness rimmed his eyes. Donna's heart bounced through her chest. Was he drunk? By the way he looked, he'd been up all night partying.

"Uncle Jamie, are you all right?" Judging by the concern in Blake's voice, he had the same suspicion Donna had.

"Barely." Grant came up behind him, shepherding a disgruntled looking Grady Hawthorne.

Jamie shot Grant a hard look. "I'm fine. We've been up all night." Jamie walked over to the table where several board members sat.

"Yeah, trying to kill my bull." Cameron stepped toward Jamie. "You got away with it once. You won't get away with it this time. Some of my workers spent the night there. They saw you walking around the pens."

"You knew where he was and didn't tell Blake?" Donna blurted the words at Cameron.

"And thanks for the help, Cameron. Having your hired hands around relieved Grant and me of some of our duties," Jamie added.

"What?"

Jamie turned back to the board. "I asked Grant to draw blood from each of these young men's horses throughout the day yesterday."

"What?" Grady stormed toward Jamie. "You had no right to do that!"

"And you had no right to accuse us of wrongdoing." Dustin stepped closer to Grady. Grady threw back his shoulders, his face defiant.

"Now, gentlemen, let's be civil." A board member took the paper Jamie proffered.

"My horse is my best friend. I'd never do anything to hurt it." Grady spat the words in Jamie's direction.

"Well, son, you have a fast horse and when you accused these two of doping their horses I thought maybe you were trying to throw the suspicion off yourself. I was wrong, though."

"All of the horses are clean." A board member passed the papers Jamie handed him down the table.

"That still doesn't change the fact you were messing around Antagonist's pen. Donna saw you with a syringe in your hand." Cameron pointed at Grant.

"We were admiring your fine bull when Donna saw us." Grant waved off Cameron's accusation. "I'm a vet. I'd never intentionally hurt any animal."

"Then what were you doing with a syringe..." Donna's mind chinked like a chute gate opening. "Oh. Dustin's horse was penned up with our livestock." She closed her eyes, put her fingers to her temple and rubbed. She was as bad as Grady.

"Right. We were trying to get a blood sample from Dustin's horse. Cameron stuck around all day, so that was our only chance."

The sadness in Jamie's eyes crushed her heart. How could she have been so careless? Why couldn't she have trusted him?

"It appears there's nothing the board needs to do." A member slid his chair back, the metal legs squeaked across the tile floor.

"There still might be." Grant raised a brow in Grady's direction. "Jamie and I kept watch on him and caught him sneaking around Blake's horse. Now we know he wasn't going to drug them. Maybe he planned to hobble the horse or mess with the tack."

"I was not." Grady spoke through clenched teeth. "I wasn't sneaking. I was out for a walk. I don't have to eliminate them because I'm better than them. I can win on my own abilities."

Donna noted Grady's defensive stance. Earlier in the week she thought he was lonely, now she saw in addition to being lonely, he used defiance to put up a wall. This young man had been hurt sometime in his life. She recognized the signs. She'd done the same thing after Jamie killed their bull and she broke their engagement.

"Do you have any evidence to support your claim?" Both Jamie and Grant shook their heads.

"Well, we can't disqualify anyone on hearsay. Why don't all of you try to stay away from each other? The Daddy of 'em All is over in less than twelve hours. Good luck boys."

Grady stomped from the room.

Jamie gave Donna a weak smile and walked through the door.

Therefore if anyone is in Christ, he is a new creation; the old has gone, the new has come!

When the Bible verse popped into her mind, shame filled every inch of her body. Jamie had changed. Her heart knew, yet her head had reasoned against it—and won. There was no possible way Jamie could love her after this. Her heart sank and she fisted her hand. The token bit into her palm. She looked at the words stamped onto it. "God, grant me the serenity to accept the things I cannot change, the courage to change the things I can, and the wisdom to know the difference." Forgiving Jamie was one of the things she *could* do.

"Jamie, wait." Donna's boot heels clicked on the polished floor tile as she hurried down the hallway from the boardroom.

The remainder of the group filed out into the hallway.

Jamie's breath heaved from him. Even though he wanted nothing more than to have Donna run to him, he didn't have the strength to deal with any more drama right now. He sagged against the concrete block wall.

The concern on Donna's face spread to her pretty brown eyes. "Are you all right?"

How should he answer her question? He blew out his breath. The flare of Donna's nostrils confirmed she smelled the booze.

Her eyes dropped from his face to her open palm. Wordlessly she held her outstretched hand to him.

His stomach dropped hard like a bull rider thrown from a spinning Brahma.

"Are you? Did you?" Emotion shook Donna's voice.

Jamie dragged his eyes from the prayer token. Shaking his head, he stared at the wall behind Donna. His mind replayed last night's events. He only had to walk a couple of blocks to find a party in the RV park. "I wanted to. I tried. I found a party, took a proffered beer and brought it to my lips."

Donna's eyes became half-lidded with sorrow. She pressed her lips together and fisted her hand around the token.

"God must have been watching out for me. Before I could take the drink another partier bumped into my arm spilling the beer down the front of my shirt." Jamie closed his hand over Donna's. "The smell curdled my stomach and soured my urge for a drink. Then Grant called me to see if I was ready for our stakeout."

Relief sagged Donna's shoulders. She grasped his hand with her free hand, prying his fingers open to reveal his palm. She placed the prayer token in his hand, then pushed his fingers down until he formed a fist. She cupped both of her hands around his.

"I'm sorry if I played a part in your temptation. I don't mean that I am to blame for your choices or sins. You alone are responsible for your actions. But I was wrong to judge you and not trust you. That must have hurt deeply.

"You have proved over and over again in the last few days that you are a changed man. The old Jamie is gone and so is the past. You asked for my forgiveness and you have it. I forgive you for any hurt or heartache you've caused. I'm ashamed of myself for my past and present actions toward you and hope you can forgive me, too."

Donna's forgiveness invigorated him, lifted his heart. He squared his shoulders and stood at his full height. "Thank you." Jamie placed his hand over hers. "I forgive you." He'd had a moment of weakness last night, but praise God, he didn't take that drink or this moment might not have happened.

"Mr. Martin."

Jamie dragged his eyes from Donna's pretty face. "Please call me Jamie."

Dustin smiled. "Jamie, thank you for including my horse in your sting operation."

Laughter bubbled from Jamie. "I hadn't thought of it that way."

"Well." Dustin shrugged. "I'm thankful you were watching out for me. You're a good man." Dustin stuck his hand out.

Jamie hated breaking physical contact with Donna, but this might be his chance to earn forgiveness from all the Greene family. "Thank you. I hope you can find it in your heart to forgive me for what I did to your family in the past."

Dustin waved a hand through the air. "I wasn't even born yet. All I know is stories. As far as I'm concerned we're good. I hold no grudge against you."

Moving closer to her nephew, Donna pulled him into a hug. Her face glowed with happiness.

When Donna let go of Dustin, she turned to Jamie and wrapped him in a hug. His heart felt so full of happiness it threatened to burst through his chest. He returned the embrace, her silky hair brushed his cheek. "I've missed you so much," he whispered.

Donna pulled back a little. "I've missed you, too."

"You've got to be kidding me." Disgust filled Cameron's voice. He marched toward them, his boots thumping hard on the floor. He pushed on Donna's shoulder trying to break Jamie's hold on her. Jamie held her tighter, turning his back so he shielded Donna from her brother.

"Forgiving him is disrespectful to our family." Cameron poked a finger in Jamie's chest.

Jamie let go of Donna. "Leave Donna out of this. It's between you and me now. I'd hoped after all of these years you could forgive. You and your dad turned your stock contracting business into a success."

"It took us longer than it should have."

"True." Jamie held up his palms. "I am sorry for that. I am sorry for the accident. I am sorry I can't remember anything about that night. Although I know there is no way I can make it up to you, I am sincere. I've regretted my actions on that night for twenty years."

Donna pushed between Jamie and Cameron. "Forgive him, Cameron. Not only to ease his conscience, but so you can move on, too. Jamie isn't the only person who's changed in the past twenty years. You've grown sullen and bitter. What happened to my happygo-lucky brother?"

"The accident." Cameron spat out the words.

"The accident changed us all." Donna grabbed Cameron's hand. "It's time to let it go. We have a second chance with Antagonist. We all have a second chance." Donna glanced over her shoulder at Jamie, hoping the love she felt in her heart for him shone in her eyes. She turned back to Cameron who studied the floor. "Jamie and I have reconnected. It may lead to a life together. I'm pleading with you, Cameron, for everyone's sake, please forgive Jamie."

"I can't."

Anger and bitterness twisted Cameron's features when he raised his head. His eyes looked past her, over her shoulder at Jamie.

"Please." She hated pleading, but this was important. She loved her brother and she loved Jamie. She wanted them both in her life. "Jamie held out the olive branch. Cameron, you need to accept it and forgive him for the accident. It happened *twenty years* ago."

The hardness in Cameron's eyes when they met hers sent a shiver up Donna's spine. Could he really hate Jamie so much?

Cameron grabbed Donna by the shoulders. "I told you, I can't forgive him for the accident."

"Why not?"

"Because I can't forgive Jamie for something he didn't do."

Donna sucked her breath in hard. The gasp echoed down the corridor. Dizziness washed over her. The room seemed to spin like an angry bull trying to buck his rider.

"What?" Her breathy question was barely a whisper.

"Jamie didn't cause the accident. I did. I was driving the stock truck." Cameron released his grip on Donna's shoulders and sagged against the concrete block wall. "Jamie passed out when he got outside. The rodeo queen helped me drag him into the cab of the truck."

Cameron's eyes, full of sadness, met Donna's. "She was with me, not him."

Donna clutched a hand to her chest. The weight of Cameron's admission caved in on her and pushed down hard, making it difficult for her to breathe. She'd hated Jamie for nothing. Lived in tormented loneliness for twenty years. Did Cameron even understand the gravity of this situation? Donna clamped her lips tight to keep them from trembling. Tears welled in her eyes and her breath released in rapid huffs. She felt as if she might faint.

Warmth covered her shoulders and blanketed her back. Jamie squeezed her to him in a comforting embrace. She wanted to look at him, see if the anger on his face matched hers in depth and fierceness. She couldn't chance it. She might break down.

"Go on." Jamie's command cut through the silence, his voice void of emotion.

"You were out cold. We dumped your limp body in the passenger seat. The gal crawled into the middle, snuggled up to me, and I pulled the truck in gear to take her to her motel." Cameron's eyes became vacant. He stared at the opposite wall. "I drove in the wrong direction. She was giggling and blowing in my ear. I wrapped my arm around her and swung the truck into a U-turn at the next intersection. I misjudged the curbs when I turned the steering wheel. The front tires jumped up on the curb. I tried to free my arm from around her shoulders. I wasn't fast enough. I turned the wheel too sharp with my left hand so I could avoid hitting the corner of the building. The cab swiped the lamp pole and snapped off the top. The back wheels hit the curb, rocking the truck. I'm sure the jerking motion frightened Old Dependable. He shifted his weight."

"He weighed eighteen hundred pounds."

Donna wrinkled her forehead in confusion as Jamie rattled off the fact.

Cameron looked in their direction. "Right. It tipped the truck over breaking off more of the light pole." Cameron's voice hitched. He brought his hands to his ears and looked down. "After all these years I can still hear Old Dependable bellow. And then silence. That's when I knew. I killed our championship bull."

Chapter 14

"No wonder I couldn't remember what happened."
Jamie hadn't realized he spoke out loud until every
muscle in Donna's body tensed. Jamie knew he wasn't
bringing her any comfort during her brother's long over-
due confession. He set his jaw, bracing for the rest of
what Cameron had to say. Needed to say after all these
years.

"Yeah, you never came out of your drunken stupor.
When the truck landed on the driver's side, your body
fell against ours. I knocked my head against the steering wheel. I ignored the pain and maneuvered around
until I could scramble to the passenger door, unroll the
window and climb out. I lay on my stomach and pulled
the rodeo queen out of the window opening. Then we
slid down off the truck. I ran around the cab. I knew it
was bad by the mess on the sidewalk."

Jamie gulped in unison with Cameron. Donna fisted

her hands, tensing her shoulders even more. Jamie ran his hands down her arms and worked at her fingers until she released her fists and intertwined her fingers with his. They all knew what happened to the bull, but Jamie's pastor instincts kicked in. Cameron needed to say it out loud, purge it from his heart and memory. "Go on." Jamie strained to keep his voice neutral and under control.

Cameron's eyes roved to everyone huddled in the hallway before meeting Jamie's. "The jagged metal of the broken lamppost." A sob caught in his throat. He shook his head, eyes lidded. "Stabbed Old Dependable."

Cameron's shoulders shook with silent sobs, letting out the torments of his past while everyone else stood in stunned silence. After a few minutes, Cameron ran his arm across his face. "The sight made me sick. I ran around the truck to the side of the building and wretched. The girl followed me. The police found us slumped against the brick building. And you on the driver's side."

Blake pushed through the group, his fist lifted. "You let my uncle take the fall."

Cameron straightened, jutting his chin out. "Go ahead, take a swing, I deserve it."

Every fiber inside of Jamie wanted to take not just one swing, but several. He knew it might make him feel better for a few minutes, but it wasn't the right way to handle the situation. Jamie released Donna and grabbed Blake's arm. Blake turned to his uncle. Jamie gave his head a small shake.

"I didn't mean to. Really I didn't." The earnestness in Cameron's voice convinced Jamie he was telling the truth. "When the gal crawled out, you were the only one left in the cab. The police assumed you were the driver. I didn't say you were. Or weren't."

Donna stepped toward Cameron, standing nose to nose. "You have lied to us all these years. You even told me it was my fault. It's my turn to play the same guilt trip card you've laid on me for twenty years. What would Dad think of you?"

"He'd think I obeyed my parent. Dad knew the truth."

"What?" Rage filled Donna's voice.

"After they arrested Jamie, I told Dad I was driving. I told him I was going to straighten it out with the police. He wouldn't let me. The guilt was eating me alive, and I begged him to let me turn myself in. He finally said I couldn't. If I did, the company would be the laughing-stock of the Professional Rodeo Cowboys Association and we'd lose the business altogether."

Donna was livid. She poked him in the chest as hard as she could. "The two of you sacrificed Jamie, his career and our love." She was so angry she trembled. "I will never forgive you for this."

Jamie drew a deep breath. Twenty years ago, he'd already have taken the first swing. Now he recognized this test of his faith. He'd vowed to honor God in his thoughts, words and deeds. Jesus didn't want his followers to judge or cast the first stone. He taught love and forgiveness. Jamie knew how it felt to want forgiveness and not receive it. Hadn't Cameron suffered enough bearing his guilt for twenty years?

Jamie closed his eyes trying to steel his resolve. Even though it went against human nature, he knew what Jesus wanted him to do. "I will, though. I will forgive you."

The horrified look on Donna's face twisted his heart at the same time a peaceful feeling washed through him.

As hard as it was to do, *and it was hard*, he'd done the right thing.

"How can you say that after what he did to you? To us?" Donna's raised voice became shrill.

"I have to forgive him his trespasses. And so do you."

"Oh, no." Donna backed away from Jamie, her eyes wide. Her anger reddened her face and she waved an arm wildly. "I'm not forgiving him. He doesn't deserve it. He's lied for years. He hurt you and me." When her voice choked she stopped talking and gave Cameron a look filled with disgust.

Swiping at her eyes with the back of her hand, she shook a finger at Jamie. "How can you forgive him? How can you? After all of the things he's done to you, said about you when it was him all along. Him who caused the accident that killed the bull."

Her eyes beseeched him. "Twenty years of our lives together are lost, along with our hopes and dreams. I wanted a family. I'd dreamed of children. *Our children*. Didn't you?"

Yes he had. Sometimes still did. Jamie nodded.

"And now it's too late. He robbed us of our happiness. I've spent my life *alone* because of him and his lie." Hurt shook Donna's voice.

Jamie closed his eyes and set his jaw. He understood her pain. He *felt* her pain. Disappointment and anger swirled through him over Cameron's confession, too. Did he want to punch him? Oh, yes, he did. Did he want to call him names and tell his peers to stop doing business with Greene Stock Contracting? Oh, yes, he did. Could he do it? Easily. Yet he wouldn't. He had to practice what he preached, literally. "I have to forgive Cameron."

Jamie opened his eyes. Shock registered on every inch of Donna's slack-jawed face. She'd obviously thought her angry, impassioned plea would change his mind. Jamie glanced at Grant.

"Why don't the rest of us go outside?" Grant had read Jamie's mind.

Blake stopped studying the toes of his boots, nodded his head and started to the door. Grant followed.

"Why don't I take you back to your hotel, Uncle Cameron?" Dustin's tone sounded unforgiving yet it was apparent he wasn't forsaking his family.

"Sure." Cameron's heels scuffed against the tile floor, stopping in front of Donna.

Donna crossed her arms over her chest and turned her head away.

"I am sorry. I know I've hurt you and I don't blame you if you never forgive me." Cameron's defeated stance turned to Jamie. "There is nothing I can do to make this right."

Jamie gave him a hard stare. "I know."

"Thank you for being a bigger man than me." Cameron stuck his hand out.

Jamie's eyes dropped to Cameron's work-worn hand. The last thing he wanted to do was shake Cameron's hand. Even though Jamie had forgiven him, he had anger and hurt he needed to deal with, to give to God in prayer. Swallowing hard, Jamie clasped Cameron's hand for a brief moment.

Glancing back at Donna, Cameron scuffed toward Dustin who waited by the door.

When the door closed, Jamie stepped closer to Donna. Other than a couple of tears trickling down her cheek, Donna hadn't released any of her hurt, only anger. If there was ever a time Donna needed someone to hold her it was now. Jamie started to wrap his arms around her.

"Don't you touch me." Donna's bottom lip trembled and so did her voice. "You're being so cavalier with your forgiveness." Her right hand flew up and chopped through the air. "He ruined your life, *our* lives. I am *furious*. You should be, too. All those wasted years."

"We're Christians, Donna. We need to follow Jesus's example and forgive. Our relationship suffered. I've never stopped loving you, but Cameron didn't ruin my life. I allowed alcohol to ruin some of it. But once I got sober, I didn't waste any more precious moments of my life."

Breathe. Her command did no good. Her emotions whirled. Words spun through her mind, twisting together like braided rope. Jamie hadn't wasted his life. The accident didn't ruin it. He bought the ranch in California he'd dreamed of and used it to give injured and retired animals a new home. He announced at rodeos, sobered up and became a pastor.

The only person who'd stopped living was she.

"Donna, take a breath." Eyes swimming with concern, Jamie touched Donna's shoulder bringing her out of her thoughts.

The air she sucked in burned her lungs. She had to get out of here. She shrugged off Jamie's hand.

"Donna, don't. I love you. We have a second chance. Don't let the accident ruin it for us again."

His fingers grazed her cheek before she jerked back her head and took a step. Her boots felt leaden again yet she managed to put one in front of the other.

"Where are you going?" Jamie's heels clicked on the tile floor.

The sound quickened her pace. She reached the door on a run and pressed the release handle down. "Leave me alone. I don't want to see you again." She glanced over her shoulder and saw hurt pinch Jamie's features. Her heart caught in her chest. The door snapped shut blocking her view of Jamie and she broke into a run.

Hot tears blurred her eyes. Each breath burned her lungs until she couldn't take another inhalation. She stopped. Bending at the waist, she tried to catch her breath. What had happened back there? Her world had collapsed and once again, crushed her happiness.

Straightening, Donna surveyed her surroundings. She had no transportation back to the RV park. Where could she go? Her breathing returned to normal and she started walking. Soon she found herself close to the FCC tent. Knowing Jamie wasn't there, Donna approached the opening.

She peeked inside. No sign of Grant or anyone else. She walked into the silent tent. Weary, she slumped onto a chair. Closing her eyes, she bowed her head and turned to the only one she could trust.

Tears ran from her eyes and sprinkled onto her blouse. *Lord, I'm so confused. Please grant me peace. Jamie's words stung my soul. Maybe I'm not a Christian. I don't think I'll ever find it in my heart to forgive my brother. I'm livid and hurt by Cameron's confession. I'm angry with Jamie about his easy forgiveness and disappointed in myself. I let an accident I had nothing to do with change my life. Please help me sort out the events of the day. Amen.*

Slowly opening her eyes, Donna's gaze settled on the keyboard. Swiping the wetness from her cheeks with her hands, she walked over to the portable piano. Uncovering it, she slipped onto the stool and began to play, finding comfort in the familiar hymns' melodies and verses. Midway through a standard, a Bible verse popped into her mind.

Therefore if anyone is in Christ, he is a new creation; the old has gone, the new has come!

Surprised, her fingers froze and held the chord until it faded into the silence of the tent. Jamie had changed. He was grounded in Christ. His forgiveness of Cameron had to be hard for him. He was able to do it because of the new person he became with his devotion to Christ.

Donna strived to have to a closer relationship with Jesus. Refusing to forgive her brother his trespasses pushed her further from Christ. She wanted and needed to be a new creation. She had to let the past be gone and concentrate on her future. The future she hoped included Jamie.

Her fingers resumed making a joyful noise to the Lord. She knew her heart and mind needed to take a lesson from her fingers if she wanted the old to be gone and the new to come.

Where could she have gone? Jamie ran after Donna, wishing he'd worn his athletic shoes instead of the stiff leather cowboy boots with hard heels. He stopped and craned his neck from side to side.

Frontier Park teemed with people. Even though she ran from the building only seconds before he did, it wouldn't take long to get lost in the crowd. It hadn't. Jamie sighed.

Grant came up next to him, puffing hard. "Do you see her?"

"No." Jamie turned to his red-faced friend. "Are you sure she went this way?"

"Yes. Blake needed to get ready for today's event. He

said he'll keep an eye out for her in case she's around the livestock or behind the chutes."

Jamie let out a snort that could rival Antagonist's. "Fat chance. She doesn't want to see Cameron or maybe any of us." Jamie swallowed hard trying to wet his whistle, quench his thirst. "I need a drink."

"Now, Jamie, don't let today's events…"

"I meant water." Jamie cut Grant off and gave him a lopsided grin.

Grant chuckled and slapped his back. "Me, too, buddy. There's a cooler of water at the Cowboy Church tent."

"That's too far. Let's head to the concession area and buy a bottle."

Grant fell into step with Jamie. His friend's presence and the knowledge he always had someone to depend on brought him comfort. Despair clenched his heart knowing Donna felt alone right now.

"Are you sure you're really handling Cameron's confession?"

Jamie glanced at Grant whose expression grew serious and nodded. "It doesn't mean I'm not angry or hurt. I missed sharing twenty years of my life with Donna, but I also have a sense of relief. Of all the times I was drunk in my life, I always remembered what happened, except for the night of the accident.

They stopped in front of the first vendor they came to and waited in line until they could order their water. Jamie unscrewed the lid and pulled a long drink of the icy cold liquid. "Where do you think she went?"

"Back to the RV park?"

Jamie rubbed his chin. "Dustin took the pickup."

"She could have called or texted him to come and get her." Grant twisted the cap back on his bottle of water.

"True, but would she miss today's event?" Jamie checked his watch. "We have a couple of hours before the rodeo starts. I know you need to report to the stock area. Why don't you try to find Dustin or Cameron and see if they've seen her? I'll keep searching the grounds."

Jamie scanned the horizon. He doubted Donna headed to the carnival area. Too much gaiety, which wasn't the mood of the morning. Heart heavy, Jamie walked through the vendor area. His eyes searched every picnic table and bench.

Fury at Cameron's actions coursed through him. All his bad-mouthing of Jamie through the years, trying to ruin his announcer career. Was that the way he dealt with his guilt? Keeping Jamie away from rodeo, out of sight out of mind. Erasing the consequences of his actions?

Pray for him. The thought tugged at his heart. He pushed it away. How could he pray for Cameron when he'd put a barrier between Jamie and Donna, again?

Stopping, Jamie realized he stood in front the concession booth where Grant bought the water. He'd gone full circle through the concessions and vendors with no sign of Donna. His shoulders sagged. He'd never find her in this throng of people.

His only hope was she'd show up to watch Dustin compete. Jamie pulled his rodeo ticket from his wallet and walked in the direction of the portal entry to the grandstand. Maybe Donna was already there.

Chapter 15

Donna wasn't in the grandstand. Only a few specta-
tors dotted the seating.

Jamie climbed the stairs to the row where their seats
were located. He dropped down onto the hard bleacher,
unscrewed the lid of his water and took a big swig. For
the first time since he could remember, he wanted something more than a drink of liquor.

A life with Donna Greene. Her last name stirred
his anger. Marrying Donna meant finding a common
ground with Cameron. Jamie told Cameron he forgave
him and he wasn't lying. However saying the words and
dealing with the emotions were two separate things.
He'd have a hard time forgetting being blamed for an
incident which cost him a fiancée and a family—and
nearly ruined his reputation.

Maybe not. A peaceful feeling nudged out the anger
in Jamie's heart. He felt the corner of his mouth twitch.

He and Donna weren't too old. If they started right
away, they could have a family of their own. Unless
Donna's health prohibited it. If it did, Jamie could live
with a family of two. What he couldn't live with was
not having Donna in his life.

He looked around the area. More people filed into
the bleachers. His phone jingled. He removed it from his
pocket. Grant texted that Dustin and Cameron hadn't
seen Donna since this morning. Dustin texted her and
received no answer.

Worry niggled Jamie's mind. Nervous, he bounced
his leg. Would she come to her assigned seat or enter
the gate and watch from another location? Should he
go looking for her? Would he find her in the mass of
rodeo fans?

He sighed, feeling helpless. What could he do?

Pray! Jamie shook his head. It was the first thing
he'd have suggested to someone who sought his pastoral counsel. He should follow his own advice. Jamie
clasped his hands, pulled the brim of his Stetson low,
bent his head, and began his petition.

Mentally singing the words of the hymns she played
refreshed Donna and chased away the worries of the
morning. She wanted a closer relationship with God.
Yet when He gave her a chance to grow in His like-
ness, she'd let her anger devour her like a ravenous
lion. Many of the hymns she played spoke of forgiveness or Jesus's ultimate sacrifice for the forgiveness of
our sins. *Her* sins.

*Therefore if anyone is in Christ, he is a new creation;
the old has gone, the new has come!*

Holding down the keys, the last chord of the hymn
faded. All week when the Bible verse popped into her

mind, she'd thought of Jamie when she should have measured herself against it.

A weak smile came to her lips. She'd held herself back from living for twenty years. No one else was to blame. She'd wallowed in self-pity so long after the humiliation of Jamie's part in the accident and their broken engagement, it had dictated her life. She took comfort in the familiar and allowed her dreams to die.

Even this week, she'd ignored the verse's lesson. Did she really have Christ in her heart? She was having so much trouble letting go of her past. She'd doubted Jamie and accused him of conspiring against Dustin. She'd lashed out at both Cameron and Jamie. It might be difficult, but she had to forgive Cameron. The words wouldn't come easily and she knew she'd have to rely on God to help her forget, but it was something she needed to do.

She owed Jamie an apology for the lie she'd told in anger. She did want to see him again, every day for the rest of their lives if he felt the same way. Donna bowed her head. "Lord, thank You for moving Cameron to tell the truth. I'm sure the words were as hard for him to say as they were for us to hear. Forgive me for not heeding your instructions and being able to forgive him. Help me to release the past and be new in You. Help me to forgive my brother. Help me to make amends with Jamie and trust You to guide our paths, whether it's together or apart. Be with all of the contestants, personnel and stock in today's events and keep them safe and free of harm. Amen."

Opening her eyes, Donna's gaze locked on her watch. She had twenty minutes to get to the rodeo grounds. Hurrying, she turned off and covered the keyboard before leaving the tent and working her way into the crowds of people in Frontier Park.

Please let him be there. Please let him be there. Donna mentally repeated the prayer with each step. She'd deal with her brother later. She needed to see Jamie now and ask his forgiveness. His willingness to forgive Cameron fueled her hope that he'd show her the same mercy.

It took every bit of her patience to get through the crowds of people who seemed to move in slow motion. Finally a break came and she could move faster toward the section where she and Jamie had seats.

Shielding her eyes from the sun, she searched the crowd. Her gaze sought and found the familiar felt Stetson in a sea of straw cowboy hats. Thankful for Jamie's hat quirk, Donna climbed the stairs toward him not letting the cowboy hat out of her line of vision. Her heart lifted with each step and rise in elevation.

A broad smile lit up Jamie's face when he saw her approaching. He stood and stepped over to allow her access to the aisle seat. Stepping off the stair, she faced him.

"I am sorry I told you I never wanted to see you again. It's not true and the opposite of how I really feel." Donna reached for Jamie's hand. "Can you ever forgive me? And not only for my actions today, but in the past, too. I'm sorry I didn't believe in you and stick by you twenty years ago. You proved so many times this week that you've changed and still I doubted your actions last night. I am truly sorry." Her hushed words rushed from her lips while she drank in Jamie's handsome features, committing them to memory in the event Jamie no longer wanted her or her family in his life.

Jamie swatted her hand away and hurt zinged her

heart until his strong arm wrapped her in a side hug. His hat brim grazed her ear. She tilted her head and rested it against his shoulder. Jamie planted a soft kiss on top of her head.

Together, they sat down on the bleacher. Jamie turned his back to the stranger at his right, creating a small shield of privacy and gently lifted Donna's chin with his fingers. He leaned close and spoke in a low voice. "I will always forgive you. I understand your anger and hurt. Even though I forgave Cameron I'm dealing with those emotions, too. I am just a man. A man who loves you and doesn't want to lose you again. A man who doesn't want the past to rule his future with the woman he intends to marry. The only way we can start fresh is to forgive Cameron."

"I know. With God's help and guidance, I plan to."

Donna's whispered reply brought a broad smile to Jamie's face, deepening the parenthesis lines around his mouth and crinkling the corners of his eyes. He tipped his head and pressed his lips to hers.

Surrendering to Jamie's soft, tender kiss, the noise of the crowd dimmed in her ears and gave Donna a feeling the world spun for only them. Her heart swelled when Jamie ended the kiss and she saw the sparkle of love glowing in his hazel eyes. "Let's continue this later tonight under the stars in the privacy of your campsite. I have a rain check for ice cream I'd like to cash in."

"Sounds romantic." Donna's cheeks warmed when Jamie brushed his fingers through her hair.

When Donna glanced at the arena, she realized the rodeo performance was ready to start. She watched the spectacular grand entry, which held no match to the celebration she felt in her heart. She had trouble con-

centrating on the rodeo and missed most the events by
gazing at Jamie. He loved her. She reveled in the happiness those three words brought back into her life.

When the tie-down roping started their attention
turned to the arena. Grady Hawthorne was the first
contender in the event.

"I think I misjudged him." Jamie ran his thumb and
forefinger across his chin. "I think you nailed it the
other day in the midway. He's hiding hurt or shame
under his tough-guy act."

"We need to keep him in our prayers."

Jamie's hold tightened on Donna's shoulders. "Yes
we do. And I need to apologize to him the next time I
see him."

The calf sprang from the gate, Grady's horse on its
heels.

"Watch his hands." Donna pointed.

Grady trailed the rope to the calf, brought it to the
ground and wrapped the pigging rope around its legs.
Grady threw his hands in the air.

"That is where he makes up his time." Jamie nodded.

The announcer's voice boomed from the speakers.
"Eleven seconds."

"Well, our boys have done better." Donna crossed
her fingers.

"Here comes Dustin to prove it." Jamie pointed to
the cowboy backing his horse into the chute.

The calf ran out of chute in a flash of black. Dustin's
horse followed behind. He swung his lasso, hit his target
and dismounted. Donna held her breath until Dustin's
gloved hands flew into the air. "Whew, his tie-down
seemed fast. What do you think?"

Jamie's sad eyes met hers and he pointed to a judge's flag.

"This cowboy broke the barrier, folks. His time is twenty-two seconds. Let's give him a hand." The announcer continued to read Dustin's overall point status.

Donna sagged against Jamie and watched Dustin throw his gloves to the ground in frustration.

"I know it's disappointing. He could still come in second or third overall at the Frontier Days Rodeo and not hurt his points ranking too much."

There were three other tie-down ropers in between Dustin and Blake. Donna squeezed Jamie's hand when Blake guided his horse into the arena. "Here we go."

Blake gave the nod and they released his calf. His quick spur sent his horse into motion and Blake into the routine of roping his calf. He hit the ground running, lifted the calf, grasped the three legs and half hitched the pigging rope in what seemed like slow motion for Donna. She could only imagine how Jamie felt.

When Blake's hands flew in the air, Jamie slid to the edge of his seat, bringing Donna with him. The rise and fall of his back told Donna his adrenaline pumped hard watching Blake's efforts. She knew Blake needed the winnings from this rodeo to keep moving on in the circuit. Dustin's loss was a minor points set back, not the financial dilemma a loss for Blake would be.

"Ladies and gentlemen, you just witnessed finesse. Blake Martin tied-down his calf in nine seconds flat. Not only is he the winner of today's events, he won the overall competition here at the Daddy of 'em All." The announcer's excited voice raised cheers from the audience.

"Yes!" Jamie sprang from his seat, hands raised in

the air. Donna brought her pinkies to her lips and blew a shrill whistle. Blake couldn't hear their individual efforts, but they continued to help the crowd roar with excitement.

Blake mounted his horse, gave a wave to the crowd and rode from the arena in a humble stance.

Jamie wrapped Donna in a hug. "I am so happy for him."

"Me, too." Donna squeezed back.

Jamie broke their embrace and pulled her to arm's length. "I'm sorry. I know you wanted Dustin to win. It's just that Blake needed the purse to continue competing."

"I know. It's okay. I'm happy for Blake, too. He's a good cowboy and a good person. He deserves a shot at the championship title at the National Finals. I'm as happy for Blake as I would have been for Dustin." Donna looked into Jamie's eyes.

Emotion deepened his hazel irises. "Do you know why? Because we're family. Our hearts have always known it and I believe it's the reason why neither of us married."

Happiness surged through Donna, welling tears in her eyes. She'd always known her heart belonged to Jamie. It was wonderful to hear that his heart had always been hers, as well.

He stuffed his hand in his pocket, pulled it free and sat down. Jamie patted the bleacher seat. She eased down onto the bench.

"I was going to show you this tonight under the stars." Jamie's voice faltered.

Donna's eyes dropped to his fisted hand. She'd seen his prayer token. Was he awarded something special for her forgiveness in his sobriety steps? By the quiver in his voice she knew it was important and something he needed to do and probably a cause for celebration. "There is no time like the present, especially at our age." Donna's attempt at humor quirked the corner of Jamie's lips.

"That's true and why we shouldn't waste one minute." Jamie wrapped his arm around her shoulders and pulled her close. "I want you to know I believe we need to put our past behind us."

"I agree." Donna searched Jamie's face for a clue of what was to come.

"But there is something in our past, I couldn't get rid of." Jamie opened his hand.

"Oh." Donna's heart jumped and she lost her breath when she saw the token lying in Jamie's open palm. It was a token, but not the kind she expected. This was a token of their love, the engagement ring she'd returned twenty years ago. "You kept it all these years." Her whisper couldn't hide her astonishment. The teardrop-cut diamond set in a wide white gold band caught the sunlight and sparkled with the promise of a new life.

"I did. I couldn't let it go because if I did I had to let you go."

Donna dragged her eyes from the ring to Jamie's face.

"I could never let you go, Donna. What do you say? Will you give this old cowboy's heart a second chance? Will you marry me?"

Tears blurred Donna's vision. "Are you sure?" She placed a hand to her chest and patted the area where she'd had surgery.

Jamie set his jaw. "That doesn't matter to me."

Time and faith had changed them both. Silently,

Donna splayed the fingers on her left hand and nodded at Jamie. He slipped the ring on her finger and kissed her.

When she could catch her breath she said, "Yes. I will marry you, Jamie Martin, and give our love another go around."

* * * * *

REQUEST YOUR FREE BOOKS!

2 FREE INSPIRATIONAL NOVELS
PLUS 2
FREE
MYSTERY GIFTS

Love Inspired®

YES! Please send me 2 FREE Love Inspired® novels and my 2 FREE mystery gifts (gifts are worth about $10). After receiving them, if I don't wish to receive any more books, I can return the shipping statement marked "cancel." If I don't cancel, I will receive 6 brand-new novels every month and be billed just $4.74 per book in the U.S. or $5.24 per book in Canada. That's a savings of at least 21% off the cover price. It's quite a bargain! Shipping and handling is just 50¢ per book in the U.S. and 75¢ per book in Canada.* I understand that accepting the 2 free books and gifts places me under no obligation to buy anything. I can always return a shipment and cancel at any time. Even if I never buy another book, the two free books and gifts are mine to keep forever.

105/305 IDN F49N

Name _____ (PLEASE PRINT) _____

Address _____ Apt. #

City _____ State/Prov. _____ Zip/Postal Code

Signature (if under 18, a parent or guardian must sign)

Mail to the **Harlequin® Reader Service**:
IN U.S.A.: P.O. Box 1867, Buffalo, NY 14240-1867
IN CANADA: P.O. Box 609, Fort Erie, Ontario L2A 5X3

**Are you a subscriber to Love Inspired books
and want to receive the larger-print edition?
Call 1-800-873-8635 or visit www.ReaderService.com.**

* Terms and prices subject to change without notice. Prices do not include applicable taxes. Sales tax applicable in N.Y. Canadian residents will be charged applicable taxes. Offer not valid in Quebec. This offer is limited to one order per household. Not valid for current subscribers to Love Inspired books. All orders subject to credit approval. Credit or debit balances in a customer's account(s) may be offset by any other outstanding balance owed by or to the customer. Please allow 4 to 6 weeks for delivery. Offer available while quantities last.

Your Privacy—The Harlequin® Reader Service is committed to protecting your privacy. Our Privacy Policy is available online at www.ReaderService.com or upon request from the Harlequin Reader Service.
We make a portion of our mailing list available to reputable third parties that offer products we believe may interest you. If you prefer that we not exchange your name with third parties, or if you wish to clarify or modify your communication preferences, please visit us at www.ReaderService.com/consumerschoice or write to us at Harlequin Reader Service Preference Service, P.O. Box 9062, Buffalo, NY 14269. Include your complete name and address.

LIDIR13R

REQUEST YOUR FREE BOOKS!

2 FREE INSPIRATIONAL NOVELS
PLUS 2
FREE
MYSTERY GIFTS

Love Inspired
HISTORICAL
INSPIRATIONAL HISTORICAL ROMANCE

YES! Please send me 2 FREE Love Inspired® Historical novels and my 2 FREE mystery gifts (gifts are worth about $10). After receiving them, if I don't wish to receive any more books, I can return the shipping statement marked "cancel." If I don't cancel, I will receive 4 brand-new novels every month and be billed just $4.74 per book in the U.S. or $5.24 per book in Canada. That's a savings of at least 21% off the cover price. It's quite a bargain! Shipping and handling is just 50¢ per book in the U.S. and 75¢ per book in Canada.* I understand that accepting the 2 free books and gifts places me under no obligation to buy anything. I can always return a shipment and cancel at any time. Even if I never buy another book, the two free books and gifts are mine to keep forever.

102/302 IDN F5CY

Name	(PLEASE PRINT)	

Address		Apt. #

City	State/Prov.	Zip/Postal Code

Signature (if under 18, a parent or guardian must sign)

Mail to the Harlequin® Reader Service:
IN U.S.A.: P.O. Box 1867, Buffalo, NY 14240-1867
IN CANADA: P.O. Box 609, Fort Erie, Ontario L2A 5X3

Want to try two free books from another series?
Call 1-800-873-8635 or visit www.ReaderService.com.

* Terms and prices subject to change without notice. Prices do not include applicable taxes. Sales tax applicable in N.Y. Canadian residents will be charged applicable taxes. Offer not valid in Quebec. This offer is limited to one order per household. Not valid for current subscribers to Love Inspired Historical books. All orders subject to credit approval. Credit or debit balances in a customer's account(s) may be offset by any other outstanding balance owed by or to the customer. Please allow 4 to 6 weeks for delivery. Offer available while quantities last.

Your Privacy—The Harlequin® Reader Service is committed to protecting your privacy. Our Privacy Policy is available online at www.ReaderService.com or upon request from the Harlequin Reader Service.

We make a portion of our mailing list available to reputable third parties that offer products we believe may interest you. If you prefer that we not exchange your name with third parties, or if you wish to clarify or modify your communication preferences, please visit us at www.ReaderService.com/consumerschoice or write to us at Harlequin Reader Service Preference Service, P.O. Box 9062, Buffalo, NY 14269. Include your complete name and address.

LIHDIR13R

ReaderService.com

Manage your account online!

- Review your order history
- Manage your payments
- Update your address

---

*We've designed
the Harlequin® Reader Service
website just for you.*

Enjoy all the features!

- Reader excerpts from any series
- Respond to mailings and
  special monthly offers
- Discover new series available to you
- Browse the Bonus Bucks catalog
- Share your feedback

Visit us at:

ReaderService.com

RS13